A GIFT OF RAGS

A GIFT *of* RAGS

ABRAHAM BOYARSKY

A NOVEL

LESTER PUBLISHING

The author wishes to acknowledge his gratitude to his editor, Bernice Eisenstein, for her encouragement and patience.

 Lester Publishing Limited acknowledges the financial assistance of the Canada Council, the Ontario Arts Council, and the Ontario Publishing Centre.

Canadian Cataloguing in Publication Data

Boyarsky, Abraham
A gift of rags

ISBN 1-895555-57-4

I. Title.

PS8553.093G5 1995 C813'.54 C95-930177-1
PR9199.3.B68G5 1995

Lester Publishing Limited
56 The Esplanade
Toronto, Ontario M5E 1A7

Printed and bound in Canada
95 96 97 98 5 4 3 2 1

For my children, who create the
chaotic medium in which everything
is possible, and for my wife, Eva.

The fallen Jew looked up at the SS officer pointing his revolver down at him.

"Now tell me, old man, who is greater, the Germans or the Jews?" the officer asked tauntingly.

"We are greater because it is you who is about to kill me and not I killing you."

CHAPTER ONE

THE WEATHER was strange. It rained all morning even as a bright sun shone uninterrupted on the Four Leaf Clover Hotel, a ramshackle three-storey structure at the southwest corner of a small square lake in the Laurentian Mountains. The electric lines emerging from the roof corner sparkled with beads of water, and on the tin panels along the hotel walls long rain-splotches pointed downward like spears.

Freda Laufer, the hotel proprietress, stood alone on the patio overlooking the front lawn and the lake. She was a woman in her early forties, with curly greying red hair and eczematous cheeks, a disappointment on what would have otherwise been an attractive face in middle age.

In the sagging bulge at the far end of the rolled-up

patio awning, a family of squirrels stirred restively. Freda glanced at the awning, then looked towards the town of St. Faustin on the far shore of the lake, quickly averting her eyes from the brilliant sun as if she'd been slapped hard on the cheek.

In the three years since her husband's death, Freda had kept her promise to him; the hotel had remained open even as her health declined and the financial hardships mounted. During the recent winter she had barely survived a bout of pneumonia. That and the polio epidemic raging in the city had depressed her severely. But now, at last, the summer of 1959 had arrived and with it the hope that the fresh country air and the preoccupation with the hotel would cure her of her ailments.

The rumble of an automobile was heard in the distance. Moments later a taxi turned into the hotel pathway. Freda stepped cautiously down the slippery wooden steps to the muddy walk. She recognized the new arrival. With tears in her eyes, she fell into the affectionate embrace of Mrs. Weinberg, an old friend and favoured guest at the hotel. They stood chatting in the rain until the shadow of the hotel completely ingested them. Confused by the sudden darkness, Freda imagined it was nightfall and quickly directed her guest inside.

The hotel was crowded this first weekend of the summer. The scent of stuffed cabbage drifted like an early morning fog through the lobby windows to the patio, where three poker games were in boisterous progress. The cardplayers, men in their thirties and forties, survivors of the war, conversed in Yiddish. Stamped with blue numbers, their forearms stirred the sultry air as cards were deftly shuffled and dealt. Dying worms slithered across the floor, vanishing between rotting planks. A cockroach crawled out of a windowsill. One of the players stood up and crushed it against the wall with his thumb, then rubbed his hands together until all vestige of the roach was erased. On the dock a boy in a red bathing suit clasped a mirror with both hands as he patiently reflected the brilliant sunlight into the eyes of the cardplayers.

The five-year-old Steiner twins were on the patio blocking the entrance to the lobby. Sprawled out across the sill, Lea played dead, and her sister Rochl, standing akimbo in front of her, refused to allow anyone near her.

Freda came into the lobby from the kitchen with a tray of cookies and coffee. She had worked hard all morning preparing for a banquet that evening. Now, dazed with weariness, the briskness of earlier years gone, she stepped unceremoniously over Lea, who was trying not to breathe, and shuffled slowly in her husband's torn slippers towards the card tables on the patio.

"Who's winning today?" she asked ingratiatingly as she went about serving the players, her wiry hair irksomely around her eyes. She swiped at the tight curly tendrils with one hand while she held the tray with the other.

"No one wins here," someone remarked in a bored monotone.

"If you're all losing, who's going to pay the bills?" Freda laughed to conceal her true concern.

"At least one of us will pay," Beryl reassured her, winking collusively to the players.

Freda smiled anxiously at the grinning Beryl Friedman—once the brilliant young Yiddish poet of Lodz—contemplating the fan of cards in his left hand.

When she was out of earshot, one of the card-players observed, between nibbles on a chocolate cookie: "She hopes we'll stuff ourselves with cake so we won't be able to eat supper."

"And we don't disappoint her!" Beryl laughed, interrupting the Yiddish song, "*Oyfin Pripetshok,*" he was humming with lyrical ardour. This tune kept him calm, but his raspy voice never failed to irritate Shloymeh Gelfand, a fruit storekeeper from Montreal, whose nose twitched with displeasure.

"What a talent!" Shloymeh exclaimed with relief when he heard Levy begin practising the violin in the lobby. "That boy soothes my arthritic knee." As he swayed his head to the melancholy strains, foam drooled steadily down from the corners of his mouth, merging under his lower lip, from where it slowly negotiated the narrow channel between two symmetric, pea-sized growths on his chin. "My Yosselle had a talent for music," he whispered sadly at the memory of his son murdered in the war, nervously fondling the coins strewn across the table in front of him.

Joseph Rosenbloom and his father had arrived at the Four Leaf Clover Hotel the night before. Joseph's recently deceased mother and Freda had been close friends for many years and so the proprietress had insisted that the boy's thirteenth birthday celebration take place in the hotel where she could participate.

By seven o'clock, the guests had gathered around two long, beautifully set tables and were munching Freda's finest delicacies with impunity. Joseph stood near the patio windows, wearing a blue suit that had grown too small for him. He was lanky, a half head taller than the boys of his age, on the verge of manhood, his voice hoarse, his skin oily, pimples rimming his brow. Slicked down with a cream, his straw-coloured hair was lustrous as he stood on a chair in the middle of the crowd under the bare light bulbs. Beryl and Freda stood on one side, his father on the other. Asher Rosenbloom was a man in his late forties, muscular, with a dimpled chin and sallow cheeks. His thick round glasses rested high on his nose. His hands were the hands of a much bigger man, cut and rough, the fingernails dirty and contused. He seemed to be uncomfortable, and periodically glanced around the room with furtive eyes, as if searching for an important item that had been lost amid the guests and the furniture.

Drawing on his dormant literary skills, Beryl took a deep breath and addressed the boy in a sombre voice.

"Joseph, this is a happy day. But for us—the handful of survivors—happiness brings with it sadness. Each moment of joy reminds us of our mothers and fathers, our sisters and brothers, our children, who are not here with us today."

A woman's sobs distracted Beryl. Moments later, when he resumed his speech, his voice was hushed but still vibrant with emotion.

"We must keep their memories alive with us. We must engrave their memories in our children and they in their children, until the blood of our loved ones is avenged. And you, Joseph, you who were born after the war, you who never saw death with your own eyes, you who did not witness the murder of your own sisters and brother, you must also remember, for you are now the guardian of our memories! You are the avenger of our dead! As this is your Bar Mitzvah, you are now a man and the promise of a man is holy. So promise us that you will avenge the blood of the six million Jews! Promise!"

Joseph was awed by the significance of what was happening. As a child he had stood at a distance from the pain and the suffering of the survivors, sheltered by well-meaning adults from a reality they felt he could not comprehend. Now, according to Jewish law, he was a man and, as a man, he was being made a confidante, one of them, a survivor, inheriting their sorrow, their uncertainty about everything except the need for revenge.

"I promise," Joseph whispered hoarsely, eyes downcast, filled with tears of resolution.

Rosenbloom pulled a long package wrapped in brown paper from under a table and handed it to his son. A happy smile spread across Joseph's face as he tore off the wrapping and shouldered the brand-new BB rifle he had so long yearned for.

As evening declined, mosquitoes drove the card-players into the lobby, then promptly swarmed after them through the lacerated window screens. But many guests remained outdoors, meticulously imbibing the cool, invigorating air. A boat sailed slowly across the middle of the lake towards the saffron horizon and from the town came the faint baying of a dog.

The setting sun drew the tarpaulin of night over the lake; it hung low from the clouds and the surrounding hilltops, sprinkled with stars. Here and there, the brief, jagged journey of a firefly scratched the darkness of the northern summer night. Lights from the hotel—distorted yellow disks—quivered along the shoreline. A bonfire was started near the dock and its resinous smoke covered the front lawn with an undulating haze, colouring the survivors' faces with ashen hues.

A small collie puttered importantly about. Now and then, it strayed too close to the flames, then jumped back into the shadows, squealing loudly.

The Steiner twins appeared on the front lawn, wearing identical red velvet dresses.

"Dance, girls!" their nervous young mother ordered, inspired by the harmonica music in the background. She shoved them into a circular space hedged by guests. With arms crossed, she stood beaming at the sight of the twins dancing to a sprightly Cossack tune. How lovely they are, she thought to herself as they bent low to kick out their fat legs in unison, their long hair flowing out behind them in a storm of curls and gold. Covered with lambent shadows, the guests huddled around the fire, touching each other, clapping politely to the rueful songs of the partisans.

Joseph watched the scene from the dock, dutifully imbibing the voices of history. He imagined the life the survivors had known before the war and the normal life from which Hitler had forever banished them. He saw them in the ghettos, in the concentration camps, in the forests of Poland. For a moment

…im across the lake, to taste
…had known, to be one of
…remony that evening were
…ere had been no need for
… of revenge out of him. He
…ntarily and with a full heart;
…do for the survivors, for the
…s and brother whose murder
… in the Baranovitch ghetto.
…he stood up and faced the
…nch-Canadian village across
…d from the clouds, then an-
…ter moon burst magnificently
…er the hills, reflected on the
…nds of amber. A gentle spray
… Joseph felt its tepid touch on
…o painful thoughts about life.
…ite about this moment—how
…aught between the murmur of
…geance and the lapping of the
…mises in a language he did not

…s had returned to the hotel, a
… wearing a kerchief remained
standing … …ing bonfire, sobbing quietly in
the darkness. She picked up a handful of warm ashes,
and let it sift slowly through her fingers.

CHAPTER TWO

EXCITED about the new BB rifle, Joseph could not sleep that night. As the voices of the cardplayers wafted up from the lobby, faces of partisans and their Nazi pursuers swayed among the shadows in the room. With his back to his snoring father in the double bed, he gazed at the open window and waited anxiously for the dawn. As so often in recent years, his father screamed out in a hollow roar the names of Joseph's dead siblings. Tormented, Asher Rosenbloom struggled to sleep even as his memories reached up from the depths of his mind to claim him.

For years Joseph had wondered how his parents had survived the war but not their three children. Even when his mother lay dying in their home, his parents never spoke about his murdered siblings.

From the intercepted glances between them, Joseph knew he had stumbled upon a secret they would never share with anyone.

Towards dawn, bursts of retching were heard from the bathroom down the corridor, then the slow, gurgling flush of the toilet bowl. Freda's voice seeped up through the floor from the kitchen below. Joseph heard water drumming into a kettle, then the loud sizzle of the kettle's wet base touching down hard on the gas burner that had been turned on in advance.

When the early morning sunlight slithered in through the window, Asher got dressed on the edge of the bed. He stood up and gazed at his son sleeping on his back. As he bent down, with the intention of kissing him on the forehead, Joseph turned away in his feigned sleep. After his father left the room the boy lay open-eyed, troubled by his feelings towards him, by the hatred he could not control and the respect he could not give. A car drove away from the front lawn. There was relief in knowing that he would be on his own until the weekend. Joseph dressed quickly and went downstairs.

The card tables on the patio were littered with cups, the sand-filled ashtrays crammed with cigarette butts, like tombstones in a desecrated cemetery. Joseph strode across the dew-covered front lawn to the dock, his rifle strapped across his back. The grass was wet and the leaves of the poplars along the inlet laden with emerald raindrops. Joseph stepped into a rowboat and pushed off from the dock. The water from the night rain squelched beneath his ankle-high black running shoes as he rowed steadily into the lake. Soon the hotel grew small, stippled softly by the morning mist. Along the shore, shadows of birch and evergreens traced a black mountainous coping.

Joseph steered the boat towards an inlet that had teemed with frogs the previous summer. The waves lapped against the rocks, breaking into a granular white foam. As the boat slid into a patch of seaweed, it scrunched over the peeling boughs of sunken birch. Suddenly, Joseph heard croaking. Then he saw them, pulsing splotches of green, crouching on branches jutting out of the water, glistening moistly in the sunlight. The frogs gazed with bulging eyes, frozen in postures of imminent leap. Joseph released the oars, picked up the rifle, and slowly cranked the lever. A breeze grained the surface of the drowsy lake, sending waves skimming through the seaweed, gently rocking the boat. He tightened his grip on the trigger, focusing on a frog about twenty feet away, then squeezed. The pellet splashed into the water inches to the side of the imperturbable frog. He cranked the lever, taking careful aim at the gulping paunch, and fired again. This time he did not miss. The force of the shot threw the frog onto its back, its hind legs wide apart. For a moment it tried to raise itself, then it lay still. Joseph prodded the animal with the tip of the oar. It was still alive. He fired point-blank into the paler green of the twitching stomach. A coronet of skin and flesh sprouted up around the wound and the frog sank beneath the seaweed.

Joseph saw the frogs as miniature Nazis, green uniforms and all, and he was fascinated by their apathy. They did not try to save themselves, nor did Joseph waver in discharging his duty to the survivors at the hotel.

At last there were no living frogs to be seen. Joseph dug the oars deep into the water, forming tight little eddies around the tips. Behind him, dozens of green carcasses lay entangled in seaweed and twigs, bobbing up and down. Overhead, a convoy of white clouds drifted lazily across the azure sky.

While the guests were eating lunch a bearded man in his forties appeared in the dining room. He wore a black jacket and a dusty brown fedora. The remnants of a large frame were visible on him, but now his body was bent, his distinguished face pale and thin. A greying beard, thick but not bushy, shielded his neck and collar. Two deep wrinkles arced symmetrically down from his nose beneath the high cheek crests to the corners of his mouth. The man took off his hat to reveal thinning hair, partly covered by a dusty black skullcap. With hat in hand, he sidled from table to table. He did not say a word, and there was no semblance of shame or self-pity on his expressionless face. An intense look flickered in his eyes, as if searching far beyond the immediate setting. His eyes unsettled the guests, intimidated many. Only Beryl refused to drop coins into his hat.

"Let your God provide for you!" he barked with such contempt that the guests could hardly believe this was coming from the genial man everyone loved.

The stranger stepped away from his table and moved slowly across the floor, a silencing nemesis of the Poland they had known. After he visited all the tables, he put the money he had collected into his pocket without so much as even a glimpse. He made his way to a chair near the back windows and sat down. A waiter brought him a plate of fried eggs and toast.

"Thank you. I'm not hungry," he whispered, although his sunken cheeks belied his words.

Beryl sauntered up to the stranger. As he swaggered past him, he knocked off his hat and skullcap with his swinging elbow, making it seem accidental. The man picked them up and calmly resumed his pose of sullen equanimity. He crossed his arms on the table and lowered his head to them.

When they were sure he was asleep, children tiptoed close and threw burrs at his clothes and even into his beard. Nurturing an old hatred, Beryl had a better idea. He found a bottle of thick dark-brown glue in

Freda's office and threatened to pour it into the stranger's beard. A number of the guests attempted to dissuade him, but Beryl elbowed them away.

"I did it to my teacher in school when he fell asleep," he boasted, as though having done it before was sufficient justification to repeat the prank now. Then, to the shocked surprise of the onlookers, he emptied the bottle into the man's beard.

By mid-afternoon the glue had hardened and the beard was stuck firmly to the wooden table. Children and adults gathered around the sleeping stranger, waiting excitedly for him to wake up. But, in spite of the loud commotion, the man slept peacefully.

Beryl's patience ran out. He raised his arms for silence, then bent down to the sleeping visitor—hands cupped around his mouth—and shouted loudly into his ear, "Fire! Fire!"

The man snapped his head up, leaving behind hardened tufts of grey-black hair on the table. Teeth gritted, he winced against the excruciating pain. But on perceiving the mocking crowd around him, he quickly regained his composure. He adjusted his hat and stood up. Nodding politely to the men obstructing his way, he walked slowly but steadily towards the exit.

In the late afternoon, Freda directed the stranger to the tiny corner room on the third floor. The low ceiling slanted down to the outside walls. She stood in the doorway, her right arm raised awkwardly in the air, grasping the doorjamb where a mezuzah should have been affixed. The sunlight filtering through a half-shuttered window in the corridor formed a grated pattern of light on the side of her head. She was embarrassingly conscious of her hair, which she had washed an hour earlier and now fluffed lightly around her eyes.

Freda was rarely able to rent this room, so it was not much of a sacrifice to let the stranger spend the night there. When he asked for the price, she muttered with lowered eyes, "For two dollars a night, we don't have to make a fuss!"

Zushe counted two dollars from a handful of coins and handed it to her.

"Thank you," he said, then stepped into the room.

"Will you be staying for a few days?" she asked shyly.

"I would like to."

"I could use an extra pair of hands in the dining hall. Would you be interested in helping the waiters clean up after meals? I realize it's not really a job for a rabbi." She gestured apologetically as she spoke, her voice modulated by a girlish giggle. "Then, of course, you wouldn't have to pay for food or for the room."

"Thank you," he whispered, but Freda was not sure what he meant.

"Then you'll start in the morning?"

"Yes."

Freda turned and closed the door. Zushe looked around the room. There was a mattress on the floor and a cardboard box with a lamp standing precariously atop it near the window. The piebald walls were peeling in broad patches. Here and there, the late afternoon sunlight exposed rectangular stains, the ghosts of furniture long gone. Zushe took off his hat and lay down on the mattress.

An hour later he was awakened by the voices of cardplayers on the patio below. It was time for the afternoon service. He stood up, donned his hat, girdled his waist with a black band he took from his jacket pocket, then turned to the east to recite the prayers.

When he finished, he took out the ritual slaughterer's knife from his knapsack, examined the sharpness of the blade along the rim of his thumbnail, then put it under the mattress. He brushed his beard down with both hands and left the room.

Two middle-aged men were playing chess in the lobby. Near them an elderly couple slumbered on a sofa. Zushe avoided the patio, where he heard Beryl's voice. He stepped through the kitchen to the back lawn. The lightly overcast sky was clearing. He followed a path to a hillock, where he had a view of the mountain range to the west. Below lay the lake, brocaded by the town lights on the far shore. The remains of a wooden wagon rested lopsidedly among the trees. A vision of market day in Baranovitch sprang to his mind. Long rows of wagons arrayed the main square, the horses side by side, munching hay, their tails swinging high in the sultry air.

Zushe walked slowly towards the town along the country road. The evening sunlight flooded the peaks of the surrounding slopes. Here and there, the scent of manure drifted across the roadway. A crow swooped low over the trees and disappeared, its anxious cackle lingering in the dusky air. To his right, the lake purled softly against the bank and beyond the distant hills a narrow, feverish horizon clung tenaciously to the day. Suddenly the sun burst into the open, releasing a fan of sunlight across the sparkling lake.

Zushe stopped near a sloping field of foot-high corn and stood there for a long time facing the lake, tracing his sombre thoughts across the terrain of decades.

He returned to the hotel through the back door. In the lobby, the two chessplayers he had seen earlier were deeply engrossed in an endgame. Professor Shpitzer and Mr. Dimant, both Austrian Jews who had survived the war years in London, noticed Zushe and invited him to their table. Professor Shpitzer bore an incredible resemblance to Einstein and even had the famous man's unruly lint-white mane. A long, solitary strand of hair meandered over his shining scalp in a vain attempt to cover it. Before the war Professor Shpitzer had been the director of an accounting academy in Vienna. Mr. Dimant, a trimmed version of his friend, was the older and quieter of the two, a man with narrow filmy eyes and of unknown profession.

The chess partners spoke in at least three different languages, each in various jargons, switching haphazardly from one to the other. Years ago the guests had stopped eavesdropping on their conversations, which frequently touched on Stalin's paternal grandfather, whom both took for granted to have been a Jew, and the famous mathematical problems posed by Hilbert in 1900. Not a thread of logic could be inferred from the dialogues of these devoted friends, but judging from the dignified manner in which they conducted their conversations, one could have easily inferred that they were constructing broad scaffolds of significant, certainly meaningful, reasoning.

This evening they seemed to be arguing in pantomime when suddenly Mr. Dimant stood up complaining of stomach spasms.

"I'll be back in a minute," he announced as he rushed off, doubled over.

Ten minutes later, Professor Shpitzer mumbled impatiently, "Why isn't Dimant coming? How long can a person sit on the throne?" He glanced up at Zushe who was studying the board and called to him, "All right then, you sit down."

Zushe lowered himself into the chair. A few minutes later Joseph entered from the patio with rifle in hand. He approached the chess game that had already collected a group of onlookers and positioned himself behind the professor. Zushe nodded to the boy, a smiled of troubled recognition on his lips.

At first, the game progressed quickly but, as time went on, it took longer and longer for Zushe to make a move. At one point, he tarried a good half-hour. When, at last, he raised his right hand, it hovered momentarily over one of his own pieces, then somehow slithered across the board, lighted on Professor Shpitzer's castle, and moved it into a position from where it perilously threatened Zushe's own queen. Uncoiling the strand of hair from his scalp, the professor twisted it with his fingers as he contemplated the status of the game. For a while it seemed—both to the players and to the observers around the table—that nothing out of the ordinary had happened. But then, as Professor Shpitzer was about to counter with his knight, it occurred to him that something was very much amiss.

"I believe you may have moved my piece," he

remarked in a drowsy intimation as he carefully lowered the strand of hair on his head.

Zushe considered the matter for a moment, then agreed that that's what must have happened. Everyone burst into laughter. Even Zushe proffered a half smile, but Joseph, who had been following the progress of the game, was convinced that the strange rabbi had done it intentionally and Zushe's luminous green eyes, glinting with mystery and pain, only deepened the boy's suspicion.

CHAPTER THREE

AFTER the guests had finished breakfast the following morning, Zushe made his way to the dining room. Louis, the headwaiter, was expecting him. He handed him a large tray and directed him to clean up the tables near the back windows. The women in the kitchen were uncomfortable seeing such a dignified man doing menial work, but Freda assured them it was only temporary.

As Zushe approached a table where Beryl and a number of guests were lingering over coffee, someone called to him in a scoffing tone: "Hey you! There's a spill on the floor!" Zushe took the mop. As he wiped away the puddle of coffee, Beryl noticed the dangling fringes of Zushe's undergarment.

"Why should we flaunt ourselves in front of the Gentiles?" he demanded, gesturing wildly, incensed.

"We can be good Jews without waving our fringes in their eyes!"

Curious about Zushe's past, one of the guests asked, "Tell me, Rabbi, where did you spend the war years?"

Zushe answered matter-of-factly, "With the partisans in the forests, then in Auschwitz. From Auschwitz I was transported to the iron ore mines in France."

"If he'd been in Auschwitz, he'd have numbers on his arm. Let's see his arm!" Beryl demanded, pouting a contemptuous grin.

All eyes shifted to Zushe to see if he would remove his jacket and roll up his sleeve. Zushe ignored the taunt and continued with his work.

"You see, I told you!" Beryl cried derisively. "He probably spent the war in Russia, on a commune somewhere, well-fed and sleeping under a feather blanket. That's why he has a beard and believes in God!"

Suddenly Zushe stopped sweeping the floor. He looked up and for a moment directed a piercing gaze at Beryl.

"Why are you here? You don't belong here! Who are you looking for? Enough of us have died already!" an elderly woman squealed in one breathless gasp, terror in the gaping eyes of her skeletal face.

Zushe nodded silently, then stepped away to the kitchen.

After completing the morning's work, Zushe returned to his room. He stood at the window reciting Psalms from memory. Now and again, he glanced down at the beach where children and a few adults were swimming. The air was scented with the smell of freshly cut grass. A row of willows along the inlet rose high above the hotel; in the open space between two tree crowns, railroad tracks glittered, disappearing in their lush embrace.

The voice of a young man drifted up from the beach. He was singing a song of the Russian partisans. Zushe stood listening with lowered eyes as he searched the past. He had survived the war with the conviction that he had been singled out for life. The miracles that had saved him time and time again from certain death were irrefutable. But why, he wondered? Why was he more worthy than his wife and children whom he had left behind in a cellar of the Baranovitch ghetto?

Mendl, a brilliant Torah scholar Zushe had known briefly in the French mines, had challenged him to believe in God in spite of everything. On the day the war ended Zushe made his decision to accept the challenge of faith. He knew that disavowing God did not alleviate the pain and only posed more questions than it answered.

In DP camps Zushe derived a meagre livelihood by tutoring children in the secular subjects he had taught in secondary school before the war. In his free time he sought out religious Jews and attended their Torah classes. In a world of ghosts Zushe assumed the mantle of an Orthodox Jew. But memories of his wife and children frequently penetrated his newly acquired spiritual armour and he could not control the hatred he bore the man responsible for the death of his family in the Baranovitch ghetto.

From survivors Zushe had learned that Asher Rosenbloom was alive. With the vague hope of finding him, he wandered through a ravaged Europe, believing that every face might be the face of Rosenbloom, that every tip would lead him to the man who had been with the women and children in the cellar before betraying them to the SS to save his own life.

Zushe followed trails through DP camps, once missing Rosenbloom in Frankfort by a day. While crossing the Czechoslovakian mountains, Zushe ran up and down the columns of weary, bedraggled Jews, seeking information about Rosenbloom. An old man had heard a rumour that Asher, his wife, and infant son were on the way to the Holy Land. In a Greek port, Zushe boarded an illegal boat heading to Palestine where a war was raging.

In Jerusalem Zushe became a Torah scholar and was often seen in musty corridors arguing fine points of Jewish law with bearded old men. One of them introduced him to a young religious woman. She was kind and intelligent, with alert blue eyes. Her father was a ritual slaughterer, who had emigrated to Palestine in the twenties. He taught Zushe the laws of ritual slaughter. Marriage was discussed but—held captive as he was by the memories of loss—Zushe did not trust himself.

One night in May of 1948, he met with the woman on a street overlooking the Valley of the Cross. The sky over Jerusalem was lit up by flares and occasional artillery fire echoed through the hills.

"I'm not for you," he whispered, ashamed to meet her eyes. "You deserve someone much better than I."

"Will you write to me?" she asked, holding back the tears.

"Yes," he promised, looking away into the darkness.

A week later the Arabs attacked the Jewish quarter of Jerusalem. The young woman was asleep when a shell struck her room.

After finishing the supper clean-up, Zushe left the hotel. From the patio, Joseph caught a glimpse of him walking along the road near the inlet. The boy bounded down the steps and quickly caught up to him. They greeted each other with friendly nods, then strolled side by side along the dusky country road. Here and there pink worms slithered over the pavement. To their right, the shimmering lake seemed tilted up towards the forest on the far shore. Long narrow bands of cloud, like a baker's stretched dough, streaked the sky, lit up along the edges by the evening sunlight. At the train station, they turned back.

On a hill overlooking the hotel, they sat down on a boulder. Zushe tilted up his black hat, exposing the broad sweep of his forehead. There was a deep dimple between his eyebrows where the smoothly arced creases on his brow dipped sharply downward like lines on a contour map.

Zushe was the first one to speak.

"I want to tell you about a man I knew during the war. Mendl Pfeiffer was his name. Mendl often talked about his boyhood days in Russia after the Communist revolution. I'm sure you know that the Russians are atheists—they don't believe in God and don't allow anyone else to either." Tiny deltas of blood vessels showed along the sides of his nose, reticulating the crests of his cheeks. "Mendl was a stubborn boy. He knew he wasn't allowed to wear his skullcap in school, but he did anyhow. His teacher was very annoyed by this and made it his duty to convince Mendl how ridiculous it was to wear a skullcap. One day the teacher stepped up to Mendl and pointed to his desk. 'Is God in this table?' he asked mockingly. 'Is He in the air? Maybe He's in the wall?'

The students burst into laughter. Then the teacher drew the obvious conclusion: 'Since we can't see Him or touch Him, God doesn't exist.'"

"Did Mendl answer him back?" Joseph asked with interest.

"He certainly did. He stood up and pointed to the teacher's mouth. 'Do you see any intelligence there?' he asked the students. Then he pointed to the teacher's forehead. 'Do you see any intelligence there?' he asked. 'No!' some dare-devil student blurted out. 'I don't either,' Mendl said. 'So it means our teacher has no intelligence.'"

Joseph laughed, his eyes gleaming with fascination.

"Was he punished?" he asked.

"Yes, but it was a blessing in disguise: he wasn't permitted to go to school for a week."

Suddenly Joseph felt he had the courage to say what had been on his mind from the moment he first saw Zushe.

"When my mother was sick, I prayed for her every day, but God didn't answer me. That's why it's hard for me to believe in anything spiritual."

Zushe took Joseph's left hand between his.

"Close your eyes, Joseph," he whispered. Joseph's eye narrowed, but he didn't close them fully. "Think about your classroom at school. Can you see yourself there?"

"Yes."

"Are you at your desk?"

"Yes."

"Do you see your friends?"

"Yes."

"It's the first class of the day. The teacher is talking. It's raining outside and drops of water are sliding down the windows." Joseph nodded slowly. "Now open your eyes." Joseph opened his eyes and saw the lights of the town across the lake. Overhead the moon lit up a patch of white cloud in the shape of an animal's face. "You created a place, a time, and people. You created an entire world, but it's not a physical world. You created a spiritual world, but it too is real, as real as your nose. So how can you say that you don't believe in anything spiritual?"

"I have to think about that," Joseph replied, pouting thoughtfully.

"Everything we see and experience has meaning and carries a message for us," Zushe said in a hushed voice, gazing with affection into the boy's eyes. "We have only to learn how to read it. When the Messiah will come, we'll see that in fact it was all for our good. God Himself will explain to us why it had to be this way and no other. Then we'll understand."

"But meanwhile we're in jail and we have to suffer," Joseph objected respectfully.

"When a woman is pregnant, she has a lot of pain,

but at the same time she knows that something good will come out of it in the future. This is the real joy, but for the moment this joy is hidden beneath her suffering. When she'll finally give birth, she'll be very happy, but it won't be a new joy she'll experience; it'll be the same joy she had all along—only now it'll be revealed." Zushe paused for a moment to see if Joseph could anticipate the conclusion of his argument, then said, "Life in exile for the Jews is like a difficult pregnancy. We're accomplishing great things every day, but we can't see them openly, so we're unhappy."

"The pregnancy has lasted two thousand years," Joseph suggested, evoking a pallid smile from Zushe.

"I'll tell you what I think but you must not repeat it to anyone at the hotel."

"I won't."

"I believe God is proud at how well we have endured the hardships. He wants to give us many more rewards when the Messiah will come, so He says, 'Go on a little longer, just a little longer.'"

"You mean He loves our suffering?" Joseph demanded, appalled.

"No, He loves how we endure it."

"What's the difference?" the boy cried vehemently, his eyes ablaze.

"The difference is the difference between seeing the world through human eyes and seeing it through the eyes of God," Zushe answered, a loving ardour in his voice. "If only we could see the world as God sees it, our suffering wouldn't be so important."

The answer was unrealistic to Joseph, but he did not argue the matter further.

When they started walking again, the swollen orange sun was setting directly in front of them. Suddenly a car came roaring down the road. Zushe moved towards the gravel shoulder, assuming that Joseph was following him, but to his surprise the boy remained standing in the middle of the road, lost in thought.

"Come!" Zushe shouted when the car was almost upon them. The boy responded lethargically and the driver had to swerve the car sharply towards the embankment to avoid hitting him, churning up a billow of dust as it went screeching down the road.

Zushe did not say a word and continued walking as if nothing had happened.

When they approached the hotel grounds, they heard laughter from the patio. Neither of them wanted to part company so they walked to the deserted dock. Over the twilight lake, newly formed clouds, tinged with bright orange shades of late evening sunlight, coasted towards the hills behind the town. In the distance, Joseph heard the voices of full-throated frogs. This was a good time to go hunting, but he very much enjoyed talking to Zushe and withstood the temptation.

There was still a vestige of light on the western horizon. Zushe took a small, blue velvet bag out of his pocket. He waited until the boy's eyes met his, then said:

"After his thirteenth birthday a boy becomes a man and he has to put on tefillin. Would you like to do it?"

"Now?"

"Yes."

"Okay, but if my father finds out, he'll kill me."

"Your father isn't here and he won't find out," Zushe assured him, the stern expression around his eyes bearing witness to how important this was for him.

Joseph nodded his consent. Zushe quickly took out the arm-tefillin from the bag. He slipped his skullcap out from beneath his hat and placed it on Joseph's head. The boy rolled up the left sleeve of his shirt, extending his arm to Zushe. After he had strapped up the boy's arm, Zushe placed the head-tefillin on his forehead. With his back to the hotel, Joseph bashfully repeated after Zushe word for word:

"Hear Israel, the Lord is our God, the Lord is One."

Then Joseph quickly threw off the tefillin, as one would wipe some slimy matter off his body, and handed them to Zushe together with the skullcap.

CHAPTER FOUR

ON A HAZY MORNING, Beryl sat on the patio under the dripping awning. The lilac mist was lifting, exposing a cape of forest on a hillside. He pulled a photograph of himself out of his wallet. It was taken in the summer of 1945 and showed Beryl standing amid the ruins of the Great Synagogue of Wilno, his right foot uplifted, resting on the remains of a pillar. He was still wearing his Russian army uniform and sported a full head of red hair. Now, as he raked his thinning hair with his fingers, he wondered if it was really him in that picture, and, for a moment, it seemed as though the photograph and the story of the man in it belonged to someone else's past, to someone Beryl had known intimately yet could no longer identify.

The noise of the children on the beach awakened

him from his reflections. With both hands, he rubbed his cheeks until he induced a tinge of colour out of his gaunt features. Now he was relatively composed and presentable. The mask was securely on. He inhaled deeply, then looked up to see Joseph standing with his rifle at his side. He hid the photograph in his wallet and stood up.

"Let's go for a walk, Joseph. I have to walk after meals. For my stomach, you know. People are not aware of a simple scientific fact: gravity is the best aid for digestion—a thousand times better than Rolaids. I noticed you like to shoot frogs. Come, I'll show you a place where there are millions of them."

They walked along the lake road, the smell of freshly cut hay scenting the air. Beryl was reminded of his father's farm near Lodz. Long hard veins stood out of his neck as he recalled his youth and his family. He reminisced about the war, the partisans in the forest with whom he had lived and fought, and about the missions he had participated in. Once he had fallen asleep on guard duty outside the camp. The rifle he was holding had slipped to the ground and shot off a round that went through his right calf. He lifted his trousers and showed Joseph the deep hole in his flesh.

Some way down the road, Beryl said, "I've been meaning to tell you about a young man I knew in the forests. Hershel Kaplansky was sixteen when he joined us. Then he wore a skullcap and had long earlocks. Why and how he came to us nobody knew. I was often sent on missions with him. We talked a great deal and got to know each other well. What a believer he had been when he first joined us, but after months of fighting and hunger, my arguments began to sway him. Eventually he shaved off his beard, then he lost his skullcap and didn't bother replacing it. Then he ate pig meat with the rest of us.

"One night, as we waited for a German train, I heard him weeping. 'What is it, Hershel?' I whispered. 'I need something to believe in,' he pleaded with me. 'You took everything away from me.' The sight of him, bent over in the darkness, touched me deeply. Tears came to my eyes. I understood him—everyone needs something to cling to. For him, it was the idea of God. So let it be! 'Hershel,' I called to him. 'You can have your God. We both know there's no such thing, but if you need it, take it! I won't stand in your way.' He was like a little girl who needs her doll. How could I have kept it from him?"

There was a chilling bitterness in Beryl's voice. The tension on his face revealed a man acting out of desperation, as if clutching one last chance to bring home his purview of life, to engrave it forever in Joseph's heart.

"The night after that he died," Beryl whispered. "He was too eager. One of our own men shot him in the back by accident." He paused, his lips quivering.

"Maybe it was me. It could have been. I have so much to tell you about Kaplansky. How wonderful it would be if you'd write a book about him," Beryl proposed. "I know you can write—your father tells me you're always writing articles. It would be a pity to let Kaplansky's memory die. Every survivor claims he could write a book. Don't believe it, it's a lie! If they could do it, they would. And that's the tragedy after the tragedy—the silence of the survivors. There are so few of us who can write about what we lived through. We remember all right, but we can't give it over. Maybe it's impossible."

"I'll try," Joseph said irresolutely, meeting Beryl's bloodshot eyes.

"You'll read it to me when you're finished," Beryl stated confidently, touching Joseph's arm with hesitant affection.

They crossed the railroad tracks, then followed a steep path, the woods humming with the sounds of wildlife all around them. A stream appeared from under a boulder and followed them deep into the forest. Overhead the sun tried valiantly to negotiate an opening between dark clouds, but succeeded only in varying the light over a range of grey, which burst into brief brilliance whenever the sun nudged the hem of a cloud.

An hour later they came to a hilltop, where they had a spectacular view of the entire lake. From there they walked farther into the woods. The path meandered through thick forest, under glittering green fir trees. They came to a grassy bluff. Beryl was oddly quiet. As Joseph's eyes met his, Beryl tried to dispel the agitated expression on his wan face. Beryl stepped to the edge and looked down into the rocky ravine.

For a long time he stood in silence, then he said in a voice as rough as the hills, "I promised to show you the frogs, didn't I? But could it wait until another time?"

"Yes, of course."

They descended to the road, then walked past a number of farmhouses, picturesque in rustic silence. From a barn about a hundred yards down the road they heard shouting. As they approached they saw an elderly farmer with a whip in his hand.

"Eat! Eat!" he yelled at a bull, whipping him across the hind legs. "He doesn't want to eat! I've tried everything!" the farmer, an old round-shouldered man with a jutting jaw, complained bitterly to Beryl and Joseph.

Beryl shook his head in sympathy. The farmer turned to the bull and whipped him again, but the bull merely swung its tail across its rump and gazed stubbornly askance.

Some way down the road, Beryl said ruefully to Joseph, "The guests at the hotel are like that bull. The world shouts at us: live, enjoy life, it's beautiful!

We'd like to—don't think we wouldn't—but we can't, just like that bull can't eat."

They walked on for some distance, then Beryl turned to the boy.

"I've seen you with that new waiter. Don't listen to him! Your father told me he doesn't like him." Frowning with contempt, he declared, "The silence of the survivors, even our sins, are worth more than all his false prayers. He's a traitor—who knows how many Jews he sent to the gas chambers?" Beryl looked away and muttered knowingly to himself, but loud enough for Joseph to hear: "Don't worry, Asher will take care of him if he bothers you too much."

Joseph replied with silence, the silence of a country evening, the silence he had already learned from Zushe.

In order to get a place at a poker table that evening Beryl ate his meal too quickly. That, combined with the hard cookies he had been munching all afternoon, triggered spasms in his sensitive stomach. By nine o'clock he was experiencing severe abdominal pain. He dragged himself to the lobby and fell onto a sofa, where he lay groaning so loudly it disturbed the cardplayers on the patio.

"It's Freda's fault!" he complained bitterly to Rivkeh, his wife, just as Freda arrived on the scene.

"Whose fault?" Freda asked uncomprehendingly.

"Who, she asks!" Beryl snarled, frowning with pain. "You disguised a piece of meat fat as a roast potato! I really believed it was a potato! It never occurred to me that you'd be so cheap! How much can a potato cost? I'll pay you the extra five cents for the potato!"

"Where does it hurt?" a solicitous onlooker asked.

"Get the dentist!" Beryl groaned plaintively. "He's my only hope."

Five minutes later, the beloved Dr. Sacks arrived on the run, the laces of his black running shoes flapping from side to side. Although he was born in Canada and hardly spoke a word of Yiddish, the dentist was a kind man, sensitive to the survivors. The guests consulted him as though he was their family practitioner.

"Are there any suppositories in the hotel?" he called out.

"We have Ex-lax," Freda replied fretfully.

"No Ex-lax!" cried Beryl, then pointed a recriminating finger at the proprietress. "You've known for years that fat is poison for me. Why did you trick me with that fake roast potato? For the few cents you saved? Here! Here's ten cents!" he moaned, reaching into his empty pocket.

"You were served your regular supper," Freda whispered defensively. Then she dared to suggest, "Maybe you ate too quickly?"

"I'm dying! If only I could give a burp. Help me!

Help me, someone!" Rivkeh knelt down beside her husband and caressed his cold, sweating hands. "It was an honour to have known you," he stuttered sorrowfully, tears glazing his eyes.

"And you'll continue to know me for many years to come," she replied optimistically.

"I'm dying, Rivkelle, I'm dying. Please try to remember me as I was before I became ill," he pleaded, although he himself could not remember what he was like then.

"Okay, we're going to do some bicycle exercise!" the dentist announced, motioning the crowd to step back. He sat down on the sofa at Beryl's feet, grasped his bony knees, and began revolving them up and around. "We're going to get your lazy colon working again!"

The dentist worked tirelessly while the guests watched the procedure with bated breath. Beryl pleaded for a pause, but Dr. Sacks wouldn't hear of it.

"Five more minutes!" he consented at last.

"A little burp—that's all I want," Beryl implored, his eyes gazing narrowly at the healthy world beyond his ken.

"Come on, Beryl, don't give up," Shloymeh shouted encouragingly. A woman offered words of support and soon a crowd was cheering him on in a loud, cacophonous roar.

The dentist's strokes became faster; he pressed

Beryl's thighs down hard against his chest until his joints cracked.

"Move back!" Dr. Sacks shouted. "We need air!"

Beryl's jaw drooped from exhaustion, his pupils lost beneath the eyelids. He was no longer helping the dentist, who was slowing down, panting exhaustedly.

"Water," Beryl mumbled.

"Water!" the dentist yelled.

A waiter came running with a pitcher of water and two glasses. The dentist paused to gulp down his glass. Beryl failed to sit up sufficiently high; his glass spilled over his shirt and he began to cry. But suddenly a look of avid anticipation suffused his face. His chest stopped heaving and a soft hissing sound was heard from deep in his throat. As the crowd held its breath, there was another hiss, clearly audible, a slow crackling, like dry autumn leaves underfoot. Rivkeh waited anxiously, her fingers over her mouth in tremulous expectation. At last it came, a resounding belch that shook Beryl's body. The crowd burst into applause. On orders from their mother, the twins forced their way through the crowd to the sofa to caress Beryl's arms. Over the years Beryl had used his belching as an instrument of war against his wife but she did not bear him any grudge for it. Now, his every belch was an opera to her ears.

"Okay, please go about your activities, the show is over!" the dentist commanded, standing on the sofa with his arms upraised, his bowed hairy shanks exposed beneath the knee-length Bermuda shorts. Beryl belched loudly as if to second the dentist's directive. With an expression of marked relief on his face, he dozed off.

When he awoke fifteen minutes later, Beryl was convinced he was running a high temperature. Dr. Sacks, who had been sitting at his side, took a thermometer out of his breast pocket and inserted it into Beryl's mouth.

"It's ninety-eight point six. Perfectly normal," Dr. Sacks said two minutes later, shrugging his shoulders.

"But my normal temperature is ninety-six point eight," Beryl whined, his face as white as an apron. Glancing up at his wife, he said imploringly, "Tell him, Rivkeh, tell him what my real normal temperature is."

In the darkness, a crippled youth of sixteen arrived at the hotel with his mother. Nora, the director of entertainment, was standing on the patio. Through her glassy, slightly crooked left eye, she noticed Gerald's accordion case and was beside herself with joy.

"Now we'll have a real orchestra for the play!" she cheered elatedly, unconsciously lifting one foot off the floor. "Levy with the violin, Sonia on the piano, and Gerald with the accordion! Oh, this is the happiest day of my life!"

"My son can only practise one hour a day." Mrs. Silvergold quickly dampened Nora's spirits. "He came to the country for fresh air, not to play the accordion night and day!"

"Of course, of course," Nora agreed sensibly, then hoisted the accordion onto her shoulder. "Come, I'll show you to your room."

Gerald was left alone on the patio. He glanced at the deserted beach, then buttoned up his brown leather jacket and hobbled into the hotel.

CHAPTER FIVE

AFTER AN HOUR of early morning frog hunting, Joseph lifted the oars into the boat, curled himself up in the back, and fell asleep. The boat drifted into a bay, where he was awakened by the sounds of splashing water. The boat was beached in a narrow inlet. He sat up quickly and saw a forest looming out of the overcast sky. Zushe stood naked in the water, his back to Joseph, immersing himself repeatedly. Rows of tall birch formed a wall behind him. Joseph gazed in wonder at the ritual. After Zushe emerged from the lake and got dressed behind the trees, Joseph stood up in the boat, his rifle at his side. There was a frog on a rock nearby. He shouldered the rifle and fired, sending it soundlessly under.

"Good morning," Zushe called. "What are you doing?"

"I'm hunting frogs," Joseph answered.

"Frogs? Are they hurting you?" Zushe asked quizzically as he arranged the fringes of his undergarment over his trousers.

"They're a nuisance!" the boy blurted out, his face flushed with righteous anger.

Zushe nodded, but Joseph read the censure in his eyes. As Joseph sat down in the boat, preparing to row back into the lake, Zushe called to him: "Can I have a ride back to the hotel with you?"

The boy nodded, although he remained troubled by Zushe's disapproval. When the boat was some distance away from the shore, Joseph said, "In the hotel they say you're like all religious people, you have no heart! You're as cold as ice! You love God, but you hate people!"

Zushe acknowledged the words with a nod but didn't respond to the charges. Joseph was now rowing furiously into the lake. Noticing the boy's BB rifle, Zushe took it, securing the butt against his right shoulder. His fingers gripped the trigger as he aimed the barrel towards the hotel in the distance, his hunched frame silhouetted on the water.

"Pooh! Pooh!" he imitated the sputter of a machine gun, standing tall in the boat, the fringes of his undergarment drifting behind him in the breeze. "One night we lay in the mud waiting for a German train. The moon stood high in the sky like a woman's earring. The attack went off as planned, but seven of us were left in the forest."

As Zushe spoke, Joseph saw himself in the forest with the Jewish partisans, a grenade in one hand, a rifle in the other, the smoke of the approaching train, rising above the naked trees, uncoiling slowly into the purple nimbus of night. The tense atmosphere in the boat yielded slightly. Zushe lowered the rifle, sat down, then leaned back on his hands. As the sun appeared from behind the clouds, Zushe saw a cluster of tiny pits on Joseph's neck. The boy was conscious of his intense look.

"You had chicken pox when you were a baby," he said.

"How did you know?" Joseph asked with surprise.

"It was in a DP camp near Frankfort."

"Yes, but how did you know?" the boy demanded, now burning with curiosity, but Zushe would not say another word.

To their right, a segment of the lake road was visible. Suddenly they heard the whistle of the eight-thirty morning express to Mont Tremblant. Moments later the train chugged slowly across their view.

Friday evening a light rain was falling on the peaceful lake. Supper was served quickly. With fruit and cookies in hand, the guests made their way excitedly to the lobby, where the furniture had been rearranged for the play Nora and her troupe had been rehearsing secretly all week.

Long strips of flypaper, crowded with hundreds of perfectly preserved flies, dangled from the ceiling over the makeshift stage. The obese Sollie Saltzman charged into the lobby to secure the electric seat, a vibrating easy chair with lacerated brown leather upholstery. He nestled himself into it, then tried in vain to extract the now crumbled cookies from his pockets.

At the back of the lobby, Freda was conversing with Professor Shpitzer. In a quaint, garbled Yiddish, he was trying to explain to her how the Dead Sea Scrolls were discovered.

"There was a little shepherd boy who was searching for lost sheep in the hills overlooking the Dead Sea," he told Freda, who was listening with rapt interest. "He looked everywhere, but couldn't find them. At last, he came to a cave. But it was dark inside, so he threw a rock into it and to his surprise he heard a clang."

"So?"

"So he knew there was something inside."

"And why shouldn't there be something inside?"

Professor Shpitzer glanced curiously at her, then went on. "After he heard the clang, he stepped into the cave, and do you know what he found? Yes! The Dead Sea Scrolls! An amazing story, wouldn't you agree?"

"But what happened to the lost sheep?" Freda wanted to know.

"Who cares about the sheep?" the professor retorted.

Freda grew sad. High on the wall behind her, the shadow of a bird fluttered mutely in the last rays of sunlight skimming over the lake.

Although she had been long expected, Nora appeared in the lobby doorway with startling suddenness. She was a tall, thin woman with short hair. She wore a long black dress, a grey kerchief cowled tightly around her waxen face. Behind her stood the actors, their heads lowered with sorrow. Nora moved ever so slowly and the audience grew silent. One by one the performers mounted the steps to the stage, then sat down on chairs that had been prepared for them facing the audience. Sonia, a woman in her fifties with long black hair and an obvious limp, stepped up to the piano and began playing softly, accompanied by Levy's lugubrious violin strains. The lights in the back of the lobby were turned off. Esther, a girl of fifteen, was the first to speak.

"Today we are all sad. Today we must decide who will go. It's so cold in this house. There's no wood and winter whistles in through the walls. I'm deathly tired, but I can't sleep. Tomorrow each family must deliver one of its own to the Germans. Who will it be? For a week we've been sitting and thinking. Who will it be?"

An idea gripped her. She raised her head and straightened her shoulders, her eyes glowing with secret resolve.

"I'm the youngest, I'll go!" she proclaimed. "I've lived the least, shared the least with the others. They'll hardly miss me. They may shed a tear or two—that can't be helped—but in the end they'll know that what I did was right. I won't leave behind children and a husband. No one depends on me. Only I can claim that! I will go! I must go! Tonight, while they're sleeping, I'll tiptoe out of the house. No one will see me, no one will hear."

Suddenly the rumble of a train was heard. For a moment, a number of the guests couldn't decide whether it was a sound effect for the play or the noise of a real German train. Panic lanced through the lobby. But the guests soon realized that it was only the CNR on its regular evening run from Mont Tremblant to Montreal.

One by one the other actors, portraying members of the beleaguered family, spoke their minds, each one intimating that the grandmother be the one to go. At last, the stage was set for Nora, who portrayed the grandmother. She raised her head slowly, her face immaculately white, and the hushed silence of the enchanted audience rolled out to her—once the leading Yiddish actress of Warsaw—like a long red carpet. Her lips parted, stirred. Words lingered in her mouth, then trickled forth haltingly, impeccably controlled.

"There was a time when a Jew thought only of life and the fulfilment of God's commandments, but now he must think of death." Her voice was mellifluously soft, yet clearly heard over the backdrop of Levy's sombre violin. "Now a Jew must decide who is to live and who is to die. Once it was Your duty, God of the Universe. Now it is ours." Her momentary silence oscillated before the mesmerized audience. "I know what I must do. I don't have to see it on their faces. They don't have to hint to an old, broken woman. I have no right to want more, I who have lived so long. Yet I do! How ashamed I am to admit it! How weak and vain I have grown, I who am a mother and a grandmother! Oh God, I am an old, old woman." She emitted a long, mournful sigh. "But once I too was a child, I too had a mother and a father and sisters and brothers. Once there was a tree in front of our house, and in the summer I sat on my mother's lap under the tree and she stroked the curls on my head and sang me lullabies. Once I was a little girl, gazing at Mother as she lit the *Shabbes* candles. Once there was a shtetl and there was a synagogue in the shtetl, and on Friday evening I sat in the front pew at Father's side. And once in a while that proud quiet man, whose face I have long forgotten, turned to me and pinched my cheeks. Then, in a blink of an eye, I was no longer a child. Mother was old, Father had gone to his Father, and I was a bride. Ephraim, my bridegroom—tall, blue-eyed, with a red beard that was the envy of the shtetl." The hint of a smile appeared on her face. "How I loved to hide beneath the yeshiva window and wait for a glimpse of my dear husband studying Torah. Then, one by one, the children came, each a special story, each my flesh, each a body to be fed and clothed, each a soul to be guided in God's ways. Each one I washed and dressed and each one I fed with these hands. Each one slept in these arms, a mother's arms."

Women in the audience were sobbing openly, but Nora was oblivious of the noise.

"Once I too was a child, a bride, a wife, a mother. Eight children came from this body. I lived for them, for their laughter. Now God has left me only one, my Raisele, my youngest. Now I am a grandmother. But who needs a grandmother? She has done what she had to do. Now nothing remains for her, nothing but her memories."

Nora stood up slowly and shuffled with difficulty to the edge of the stage. She glanced one last time at her family, then turned the knob of the phantom door.

The audience burst into loud applause. The performance was over but oddly Nora was still weeping. The rest of the cast lined up at the front of the stage and took one bow after another. Amid sorrowful voices, children were screaming from exhaustion. Dazed by the performance, the guests stood about in stunned disarray. Suddenly, the sounds of an accordion were heard. Gerald was standing in the middle of the stage, his mother at his side, his long delicate fingers fashioning a sprightly tune. The guests were slow to respond, but soon chairs were pushed aside and a circular space coaxed out of the crowd. Two women jumped into the middle, their arms swinging wildly to a bellow of joyous endorsement. Others joined the dancing. Ignoring the flatulent signs of an imminent stomach attack, Beryl was embraced with a bandy-legged old man as they waltzed recklessly around the floor. Sollie sat stuck helplessly in the vibrating chair, winking coyly at the women dancing around him, a swarthy flush on his flaccid face. Even as the music played, the glossy tracks of tears smeared a cheek here and there.

The family of squirrels nesting on the patio awning had become an intolerable nuisance of late. Although the cardplayers were oblivious of their excursions up and down the patio wall to the awning, the squirrels terrified the children. Just before lunch on the second

Sunday of the season, while Asher Rosenbloom sat on the patio reading the Jewish daily *Forward*, a squirrel jumped down near him, triggering panic among the children and women. Freda appeared on the patio with a broom. Rosenbloom grabbed it from her and started beating the underside of the awning. Two adult squirrels scurried out and three tiny squirrels came tumbling down onto the patio in a torrent of twigs and dried leaves. The adult squirrels went clambering up towards the hotel roof while the babies squirmed about blindly under the card tables. One of them rolled off the patio onto the stones below. Another crawled towards the twins. Moving to protect them, Asher stepped on the tiny squirrel, crushing it beneath his heavy work boot. With one sweep of the broom, he flung the oozing mass of scarlet and grey off the patio. The third baby crawled towards Freda, who was screeching hysterically. Rosenbloom turned around and kicked the squirrel against the wall.

Meanwhile the mother had returned to the scene. She rolled up the bleeding body of the squirrel that had fallen off the patio and carried it between her teeth to a nest on a willow bough in the front lawn. Then she came for the baby on the patio, which lay squealing quietly amid leaves near the wall. Rosenbloom was waiting for her with a broom. Swiping at her, he forced her repeatedly to retreat.

"Let her take the baby!" Freda cried from the lobby doorway as she watched with anguish the mother's desperate attempts to save her offspring.

"Let her!" Rosenbloom shouted in a sudden change of mood.

Furtively eyeing her surroundings, the squirrel searched the heaps of leaves on the patio floor. She found the baby, but the squealing had ceased. The mother left the patio alone.

Rosenbloom approached Joseph who had watched the events unfold from the corner of the patio.

"Don't think it didn't hurt me to do it," he said. "Don't think I didn't see my own murdered children before my eyes."

Shloymeh and Zushe were standing on the dock from where they had witnessed the violence on the patio. A fly was tickling Shloymeh's neck and another was playing musical chairs with the growths on his chin. He did not bother to brush them away, nor to wipe the tears streaming down his ruddy cheeks.

Zushe was nodding pensively, trying to understand something.

CHAPTER SIX

ALTHOUGH Zushe's overt orthodoxy was a cause of controversy, Freda—usually sensitive to matters that might jeopardize hotel income—braced herself stubbornly for the worst. With singular composure, she brushed aside repeated complaints and even threats of early departures.

Certainly some guests were annoyed by the strange rabbi, by the fringes of his undergarment he seemed to flaunt at them, by his unflinching faith in God, which they interpreted as a callous evasion of their recent tragic history. But at the same time the other side of Zushe was being felt throughout the hotel. He was a treasure house of fascinating information. His friendly, candid gaze distinguished him from all the guests and even endeared him to some who could not conceal their distaste for religion. His solemn deportment expressed an inner, measured calm, a self-confidence, a seeming acceptance of the past they admired although they could not comprehend. To whomever he spoke he brought a sense of tranquillity, an interest in non-materialistic matters.

The friendship between Joseph and Zushe was taking firm root. Joseph found Zushe to be dependable, always willing to listen and to help, not only with advice, but in real practical ways. He symbolized a new perspective on life. For the first time, Joseph had met an adult who behaved like an adult, who was rational and calm, who acted in a way that was consistent with his beliefs. For the first time Joseph did not feel that he had to serve adults, either by obeying them or by being an instrument for their memories. For the first time someone paid attention to him, not as a child but as a person with intelligence and independent character. In this warm intellectual environment Joseph began to feel he had worth as a human being, not merely as the son of a survivor, an additional limb to experience his father's pain.

Early one morning, while most of the guests were asleep, Joseph walked down to the beach holding his rifle over his shoulder. Zushe was standing near the dock. As Joseph approached him, he began marching away along the shore, his hat angled high over his brow to shield his eyes from the bright morning sunlight. Without a word of greeting, he counted his pace out loud.

"Thirty-two, thirty-three . . ."

Joseph didn't understand why Zushe was following the shoreline so closely, soaking his shoes and socks in the process.

"Two hundred and seventy-three feet!" Zushe announced. With his eyes lowered to the ground, his earlocks fell forward around his ears and from time to time he swept them back with his fingers.

At the far end of the beach, where the inlet met the road, Zushe turned, megaphoned his hands around his mouth, and called out, "Three hundred and forty-eight feet in total."

On his way back to the dock, he walked differently, one foot in front of the other, the heel of the front one touching the toe of the other. Painstakingly, he followed the shape of the shoreline towards the dock, his arms outstretched for balance like a tightrope walker, all the while counting out loud, not daring to look up lest he lose the tally.

"Six hundred and seventy-two feet!" he called out as he approached the dock. He looked up at Joseph and asked rhetorically, "How can the same shoreline be twice as long?" Joseph was indeed surprised and eagerly anticipated Zushe's answer, which came at once: "If I would use my little finger to measure length, the shoreline would be more than a mile long, because then I could follow every little curve in and out. And if I use the tip of a pencil, it would be hundreds of miles long. You see, Joseph, the length of the shoreline depends on how we measure it."

"What are you trying to say?" the boy asked spiritedly, sensing from Zushe's voice that an important point had been made which he did not fully understand.

"The shoreline looks like it's finite in length, but that's only an illusion. Each piece of shoreline is really infinitely long." Zushe hesitated, allowing the boy to think for a moment, then went on. "And it's the same with all of creation. On the surface, everything looks finite—that's how God created it—but the truth is that inside all that we see and all that exists is infinity."

"You mean everything is God?"

"Of course, dear Joseph," he replied matter-of-factly, unable to restrain a smile. "And even a frog is much more than just a frog. It's really a piece of infinity."

One pleasant afternoon Zushe found Joseph in the back lawn sitting on a wooden swing tied to a bough of an old oak. He sat stooped over in thought, leaning to one side, swinging slightly back and forth as he dragged his running shoes through the sand, unaware that Zushe had approached and was now standing behind him. Zushe pushed the seat gently forward. With a backward glance, the boy acknowledged Zushe's presence. Because he sat crookedly on the swing, it swerved from side to side as it arced back and forth. But, strangely, even as Zushe's push came with identical force, the swing moved erratically, all over the place, refusing to settle into a steady pattern of motion.

When, at last, Zushe let the swing decelerate, Joseph jumped free to the grass. Zushe tried to explain the physical phenomenon.

"There was no repetition in the pattern of swings. No two arcs were the same or ever would be," he said. "The motion of the swing is infinitely complex just like the shoreline of the lake is infinitely long. The infinite is everywhere—we only have to open our eyes to see it."

That evening they walked into the forest behind the hotel. When they were a good distance away, they began playing a game Zushe had made up. Joseph would say any word that came to his mind and Zushe would explain it in Torah terms.

"Tree," Joseph prompted.

"Wood to heat a room where a little boy is studying the *aleph-bais*," Zushe explained, nodding cheerfully.

"Water."

"Water flows from a high place to a low place, like Torah knowledge, which moves from the lofty intellect to the lowly emotions in order to guide them properly."

"Leaf."

"Even the seemingly purposeless turning of a leaf deep in the forest is the direct will of God. He desires that movement and not only that—He also shapes the drop of dew on the leaf."

Now and then, as they followed the narrow trail, Zushe would bend down and pick up a twig. Joseph didn't understand what he was doing, but by now the boy knew him well enough to suspect that even from this innocuous activity there would be something to learn. When they finally reached the top of a hill, Zushe was holding a handful of twigs between eight and twelve inches long.

They sat down on a boulder. Zushe gave Joseph one of the twigs he had collected and asked him to break it. The boy took it with both hands and bent the twig easily until it snapped. Then Zushe handed him the entire bundle.

"Break them," he said.

Joseph tried but he couldn't bend the bundle, not even slightly. Grinning, he gave it back to Zushe.

"When a Jew denies his identity, he stands alone; he's like a single twig. Anything at all can break him. But when he lives as a Jew, in a Jewish community, with the laws of Torah to guide him, nothing in the world can harm him."

Joseph admired Zushe, but he wasn't yet prepared to commit himself to his ideas. Deeply influenced by the horror stories of the survivors, he resisted the tenor of Zushe's arguments. Now, as he sat beside him, the air scented with pine, evening sunlight mottling the damp earth around their feet, the boy pondered Zushe's theory of Jewish invincibility. If only the war hadn't provided six million counter-examples.

"Hitler showed the world that we can be easily killed, that we're not really important. Look at us, we're only a few million left among billions. Aren't we conceited to believe we're so important!"

Zushe had an immediate answer.

"There's a chemical in the body called insulin. It weighs less than a gram in total, but without it the human body couldn't survive more than a few days. Should we say insulin isn't important because it's small in quantity? Joseph, Jews are the insulin of the human race." There was a momentary silence, then Zushe said whisperingly, "When the Greeks destroyed our Temple in Jerusalem two thousand years ago, there were rabbis who wanted to delete the word 'powerful' from our daily prayers in reference to God. How could God be powerful, they argued, if He stands idly by and watches the enemies of Israel desecrate the Temple. But when the rabbis thought the matter through carefully, they realized that God's silence was the greatest proof of His might. Which father can stand by and let his children be beaten? No human father. Only God can do it."

"But why should He want to?" Joseph asked simply as his thoughts riffled through the grievous books of Jewish history.

"Perhaps the Jews had sinned, Joseph? It hurts me to say this, but maybe we had to be punished. Not because God wanted to punish us, but because we had to be educated, just like a child has to be educated when he runs across a busy street."

It had begun to rain and water was dripping from a tree into Zushe's hat. He looked with affection into the boy's eyes as Joseph thought about the school year that awaited him. He wanted to speak to Zushe about his plans for the future. Grade nine was an important year and he had to make major decisions. In spite of his penchant for literature, he had decided to take the science option in the spring—three mathematics courses, physics, and chemistry. There would be little time for reading and sports. After high school there was university, then a career, marriage, and all that. He would do exactly what all his friends were doing, exactly what had been planned for them by parents who had just barely survived the war. For these parents there were no luxuries and the Torah path that Zushe symbolized was a luxury, for some a deception that had cost them their families and their souls. They were not about to let their children take that route, which led to poverty and likely death at the hands of future Nazis.

But Joseph was eager for knowledge and Zushe was showing him another way, a way that circumvented high school and university and went directly to the wellsprings of wisdom. How he wanted Zushe to take him to Jerusalem, to a yeshiva, where he would sit and learn the Torah all day. If only he had the courage to follow his instincts! But he knew his father would not consider it for a moment and it would only make him angry for a long time.

Zushe's voice congealed out of the darkness.

"Joseph, everyone thinks that God is evil, that He's a big man with a big stick in His hand, and that if someone sins, He's quick to beat him. The truth is that man makes himself dirty, and God merely washes him clean."

Suddenly tears welled up in Zushe's eyes and, even as Joseph observed him closely, he could not suppress an expression of pain on his face.

It drizzled most of Saturday. In the late afternoon, when the rain finally let up, Joseph stepped out to the patio with two towels and a writing pad. One towel he used to dry a corner of a table and the other he placed on a wooden chair to sit on. For a few days now he had been thinking about the annual children's literary contest, which was two weeks away. He considered the idea of writing about Beryl's friend Kaplansky, but he was afraid that Beryl would be too critical and so decided to write a story he had overheard from one of the guests the previous week. When he had completed the first paragraph, Asher appeared on the patio holding a heavy bag in his hand. Joseph knew it was the change from the cash register which he had to roll up for the Monday morning deposit at the bank.

"What are you doing?" Asher asked, then leaned over Joseph's shoulder with narrowed eyes as if to decipher the small English script he could not read anyhow.

"Just scribbling something," Joseph replied indifferently.

"For the waiter?"

"Which waiter?" The boy looked up curiously.

"The one who pretends to be religious," his father retorted with anger.

Joseph did not think of Zushe as a waiter.

"He makes you believe he's your friend. I know his type. I can look at a person and see right through him. I was in the NKVD. He says one thing and means another. He wants something from you. I want you to stay away from him." Asher raised his hand as if to place it on the boy's shoulder in a gesture of fatherly affection. "I know you've run short of BBs. I'll bring you ten packs Friday night."

Early Sunday morning, while most of the guests were still sleeping, Zushe met with Joseph in the dining room. Zushe opened a holy book and began to speak.

"This Talmud is called *Baba Kamma*. It deals with damages to property and with the persons who bear responsibility for those damages. On this page, there's an interesting case."

The guests who appeared were surprised by the sight of Zushe studying Torah openly with the boy.

"Go ahead," Joseph said, sitting somewhat uneasily at his side. "I'm listening."

"Suppose a person is standing on a roof and he throws down a glass vase. Another man, who is on the ground below, smashes the vase with a stick just before it hits the ground. Who's responsible for the damage? We may think that the man on the roof is liable because he threw the vase down and it was inevitable that it would break. But clearly the man who struck it with the stick is the one who actually broke it. So who is responsible? It's not so obvious, Joseph. After considerable arguing back and forth, the Talmud concludes that the man on the roof is liable."

Professor Shpitzer sat facing Zushe, arms folded across his chest, listening, but pretending to be disinterested. Suddenly Rosenbloom entered the lobby.

Silence gripped the men huddled around Zushe and the boy. Joseph looked up and saw his father approaching. Zushe felt Asher's proximity and braced himself instinctively for an attack. Breathing shallowly, he continued speaking as the guests moved aside to afford Rosenbloom a direct view of his son and Zushe.

Zushe went on: "The Talmud now considers the case where a man throws a child down from the top of a roof and someone else standing below kills the child with a sword. Unlike the case of the vase where we were dealing with an object, the rabbis prove that the one who slayed the child with the sword on the ground is guilty of murder because the child was alive when the man at the bottom slayed him. A miracle could have occurred at the very last second and the child would have survived." Zushe paused, pensive, then continued in a quiet voice. "From this we understand how much the rabbis believed in miracles and the sanctity of every second of life."

Zushe caught a glimpse of Asher listening. Indeed, he had moved close and stood peering over his son's shoulder at the book they were studying. But suddenly Asher threw a derisive glance at Zushe, turned sneeringly and, with a click of his tongue, strutted away.

CHAPTER SEVEN

Monday morning, a group of guests milled about on the front lawn under a bright, warm sun. Beryl had grown tired of the poker game and stood up to stretch his legs. Looking towards the inlet, he noticed Sollie near the road, pacing back and forth in his wide, waddling gait while he waited for his taxi ride into town.

Beryl's stomach problems had made him lose thirty pounds in the last two years, and now he envied Sollie his every ounce. Each summer, before checking in at the Four Leaf Clover, Sollie stopped off at the National Bank in town to deposit his money. He kept only a few dollars in his pocket and whenever he needed more—either to tip a waiter or to buy chocolate at the canteen—he took a taxi into town and withdrew the necessary cash. Often the cost of the taxis exceeded the amounts withdrawn, but Sollie had no choice; wheezing and sweating as he listed from side to side, he could hardly shuffle across a room, never mind walk the mile and a half to town. It was his awkward gait that made it so difficult; with feet spread wide apart, hands open and turned clownishly upward at his sides, it appeared as if he was crawling along an invisible wall that was constantly receding from him.

Beryl had made it his duty to admonish Sollie for his absurd habit: Sollie should either keep his money with him or find a less expensive way of going to and from the bank. Cycling, for example. Whenever Beryl mentioned the bicycle, the good-natured Sollie would burst into loud, rollicking laughter.

Now, on noticing Beryl walking towards him, Sollie couldn't repress a shudder that radiated from head to foot. Glancing desperately, he searched for a place to hide. Sollie's round, puffy face was like a face seen through a magnifying glass and whenever Beryl looked directly at him—no matter how much pain he was in—he could not refrain from smiling.

Without a word of greeting, Beryl began to administer his familiar advice: "Never mind the money you'd save, just think of your health! Look at that bicycle over there! You'd lose a hundred pounds the first month if you cycled into town regularly!"

"A hundred pounds!" Sollie laughed incredulously

as the hot morning sun beamed off his sweating brow.

"I guarantee it in writing!" Beryl promised, biting his lower lip to keep from laughing.

"We'll see, we'll see," Sollie replied evasively.

"That's what you've been saying since 1954, and all I see is this!" he exclaimed, poking his forefinger deep into the tight, massive orb that was Sollie's abdomen.

"The taxi will be here any second," Sollie said, eyeing the road anxiously.

"I cancelled it."

"You didn't!"

"I did it for your health, Sollie."

"Why, Beryl? Why?"

"This summer is going to be different, Sollie. I don't want you to pop off with a heart attack. You survived Hitler, do you want to be killed by your own weight?"

"I'm healthy, Beryl. Believe it or not, I really am."

"Bring the bike here!" Beryl called to Joseph who happened to be standing near the inlet. Joseph took the rusting old bike that lay under the patio and walked with it to Beryl.

"Come with me," Beryl said. He crooked his arm around Sollie's and led him up the road which looked down upon the shore of the lake as it meandered towards the town. "It's downhill all the way," Beryl assured him, gesturing smoothly downward with his hand.

"What about getting back?"

"I'm going to run at your side into town—I could use the exercise—then I'll ride the bike back," Beryl promised. "It's all planned out."

Resigned to his fate, Sollie lumbered after Beryl to the top of the hill.

"But it's impossible! It's impossible!" he stammered, as if in a last-ditch effort to save his life.

"Nothing is impossible. All you have to do is mount the bicycle. Like this. I'll hold you as you go. Come on, Sollie, let's not waste time—the bank is closing in twenty minutes."

In full view of the guests on the front lawn, Sollie raised his right leg, but his foot barely reached the pedal.

"Bend your knee," Beryl instructed him, showing him how.

Sollie did as ordered and with Beryl's help managed to clear the bar. But suddenly there was a loud noise as Sollie's khaki shorts burst along the side seam.

"It's nothing, absolutely nothing," Beryl assured him, gazing bemusedly at the foot-long tear through which a balloon of flesh had emerged.

That was the least of Sollie's problems; even as he stood on his tiptoes, the bar was jammed painfully into his groin.

"Put your left foot on the pedal!" Beryl shouted,

straining to keep Sollie balanced on the bike. "Not the right one! The left one! There, you did it!"

Now Sollie's full weight rested on Beryl as he strained to keep the bike from toppling. Groaning miserably, Sollie inadvertently pushed the pedal and the bike started rolling down the hill. With his left hand on the handlebar, his right arm ineffectually around Sollie's back, Beryl loped along, but after a few seconds he was unable to keep up with the accelerating bike and had to let go. The bike swayed from side to side as it snaked down the road gaining speed. Sollie released the handles, his legs and arms splayed helplessly outward as the bike sped past the inlet towards the lake. There was a crash and Sollie went rolling down the escarpment towards the rocky beach.

Beryl hobbled to the scene, clutching his abdomen with both hands.

"Are you all right, Sollie?" he asked with genuine concern.

Sollie did not answer. Spurning Beryl's outstretched hand, he rolled himself into an upright position. He was covered with pebbles and earth, his clothes torn. Badly bruised, Sollie staggered towards the hotel.

Freda and Zushe had witnessed the scene together through the dining-room windows overlooking the front lawn. Zushe was unable to restrain a smile when Sollie had careered chaotically down the road. On noticing Freda looking at him, he covered his mouth with his hands, embarrassed, as if to deny that he had smiled.

"It's wonderful to see you smiling," she remarked happily.

"I hope he's all right."

"They're already walking back. Do you realize this is the first time I've seen you with a smile? Your face looks so different when you're happy. You should smile more often. It doesn't cost anything." Zushe smiled again. "Good, good. And you're making me happy also. Isn't it a commandment in the Bible to make another person happy?"

"It is," he assented, grinning.

No matter what Freda was doing, part of her was constantly on the lookout for Zushe. There was a sprightliness in her gait and she was frequently visibly happy. The previous summer, a guest had given her a bottle of perfume. Now she bothered to find the unopened bottle and daubed the perfume on her neck, a little too heavily perhaps, and examined herself girlishly in the door mirror of her room behind the kitchen.

Memories of her youth and the war years in Asian Russia now stirred in her feelings she had long forgotten. The excitement of those years, the energy with which she had tackled any task, filled her with a pride she needed in her budding relationship with Zushe.

Freda had never viewed herself as an intellectual. From an early age she knew she wouldn't be successful in school. Her strength lay in her ability to work hard, to devote herself honestly and fully to the task at hand. She had a love for physical activity. After arriving in Uzbekistan with thousands of other Jews from Poland, she was placed in a munitions factory. There she felt perfectly at home. Nothing was too hard for her, no quota daunted her. She worked eighteen-hour shifts, carrying live ammunition from a depot to the shell assemblers, cherishing every moment. Here her qualities were recognized as virtues. She blossomed in the factory, oblivious to the endless chatter about ration cards.

In a short while, she had become a celebrity. "Freda Medresh has produced 240 per cent times her quota!" the official government poster proclaimed. "Russia is proud of this young woman!" Beneath the inscription, a large photograph of an attractive young woman smiled blissfully at the world. This poster hung on the walls of every factory in Uzbekistan until the end of the war.

One day someone left a bicycle lying across the entranceway to the factory. Thousands of workers stepped right over it, or walked around it, but no one bothered even to push it aside. No one except Freda. She lifted it up and rested it against a nearby wall. The director of the plant—a talented young engineer from Moscow—had observed the scene from his third-floor window. He ran down the stairs, found Freda, and exclaimed, "Because of you, Russia will win the war!" The next day he made a proposal of marriage. Blushing, Freda stammered, "You're educated, an engineer, an intellectual. I'm a simple country girl. I never even finished gymnasium. I'm no match for you. People will laugh at you." Had he been a Jew, his insistence might have convinced her in the end, but she held firm and he eventually accepted her decision.

In the tense atmosphere of wartime Russia, where each moment was a moment snatched from illness and hunger, young women and men lived greedily. There was no time to develop friendships. A young couple would often be on intimate terms short hours after meeting. Whereas her friends gave themselves freely, Freda, in utter simplicity, was looking for a stable relationship that would be the solid foundation of her life. She would settle for nothing less.

At a party celebrating the Russian Revolution, Freda saw three young men standing with a group of Jews from the factory. These men had recently been freed from a Siberian prison. One of them had thick black hair and a badly pimpled face. Her heart gave a leap. This is the man I will marry! she said to herself. Perhaps it was her sense of inferiority that drew her to him, astutely balancing her intellectual inadequacies against his physical deficiency. Someone physically and intellectually attractive would not want me, she reasoned. Although it seemed like an act of self-preservation, she knew she would eventually love him. Freda's friends tried to dissuade her: "You're a beautiful young woman and he's just a mass of festering pimples!" But Freda's mind was made up and she shrugged off their objections with a happy, confident smile.

Gershom Laufer was a dreamer, an artist, a dilettante in almost every intellectual endeavour undertaken by man. With his university education interrupted by the war, he felt cheated. If not for Hitler, he would have become a man of letters, a philosopher, a professor at a university. The resentment he harboured for his lost opportunities coloured his every thought and action. Freda was forever in awe of the breadth of his knowledge and his articulate speech. She loved him, seeing in him all that she was not, but she would not let him touch her until the night of their wedding—that much she remembered from her saintly mother whom she had left behind in the Ukraine.

When the production quotas were doubled in the autumn of 1943, Freda took the lead in the factory. Leaping deftly from platform to platform with fifty pounds of TNT in her arms, she set a magnificent example for her fellow workers. One day, as she ran down a corridor, her knee struck a rusty nail sticking out of a wall. Almost a month went by before she admitted that she was ill. By then the infection had spread down her leg and she could hardly walk. Limping, she trudged around the factory, wincing with pain. She could not eat and lost twenty pounds. Only when the plant manager ordered her to seek medical help did she leave her job. But the doctors weren't able to halt the raging infection. On a bitterly cold night in November, Laufer bundled up his wife in a blanket and carried her through the town to the train station. They boarded a train to Samarkand. In the morning, he carried her to the main hospital. In the emergency room, he pressed the attending doctor against a wall. "Save her or I'll kill you!" he commanded. Defying every prognosis, Freda began to recover. In a month, she returned to the collective farm, but she didn't go back to the factory. She worked as a seamstress and waited eagerly to conceive a child. She waited but the child did not come.

They arrived in Canada in October 1952. The boat landed in Quebec City. For years she recalled vividly the train ride to Montreal, the scenic French-Canadian villages, the cars packed with survivors poised sombrely for a new life. Once in Montreal, Gershom Laufer found work at a Yiddish daily newspaper, the *Canadian Eagle*, but not as a writer or even as an editor. The newspaper needed a night typesetter and so, Gershom—deeply disappointed with life—learned to typeset. But in his heart he yearned to work at his beloved vocation of writing. One night when there was not enough copy to fill a page and the editor was inaccessible, Gershom took the liberty of inserting a short article of his own. It was an interview with a famous rabbi he had done in a German DP camp just before setting off for Canada. Although well written and interesting, its unavoidable religious overtones aroused the ire of the leftist editor, who, in line with Communist dogma, disapproved of anything that smacked of religion.

And so Laufer was without a job. In the spring of 1953, Freda came across an advertisement for a hotel in the Laurentian Mountains. If they could earn enough money during the summer months, Gershom would have free time to pursue his writing career the rest of the year. There was nothing she wanted more than to see her husband happy and fulfilled. Of course, it would require a great deal of work and, of course, she would have to carry most of the burden, but it was the least she could do for the man she loved, for the man who had saved her life in Russia.

Although initially neither Freda nor Gershom knew anything about running a hotel, Freda's talent as a cook and devotion to duty quickly made the venture a success. Somehow Gershom was able to find blocks of time to seclude himself in unoccupied rooms and began work on his magnum opus, a three-volume novel depicting life in Poland between the wars. The hotel became Gershom's life—through it he relived his memories of the intellectual life he had known before the war. The street life of Warsaw was re-enacted in the Four Leaf Clover Hotel. Literary meetings were convened every Friday night in the lobby and every second Wednesday evening political symposiums on the state of Israel were conducted in the presence of experts Gershom lured to the hotel with promises of expense-free vacations. Under Gershom's gentle guidance, the hotel's reputation spread quickly through the burgeoning Jewish communities of Montreal and New York and by the third season the hotel was completely booked months in advance.

Money was no longer a problem, but Freda was approaching forty and she was still childless. She tried to conceal her desperation from Gershom, but he was sensitive to her envious glances at children in the hotel. His self-blame found expression in ever worsening chest pains. An acute heart condition was diagnosed. Over the course of a year his life ground to a halt. In May 1956 Gershom Laufer died silently in his sleep. His suffering and his dreams had come to an end. It was only the hotel that kept the widow functioning in the ensuing weeks. The emotions she had lavished on Gershom she now drew back into herself, not to be shared with a world that did not know her, that would judge her only by appearances, not for who she really was.

But Zushe's presence in the hotel changed her image of herself. Once again she felt needed and useful to another human being—not only as a cook and a manager, but as a woman. And she was not ashamed of her reawakened feelings. Certainly Gershom would not have expected her to live the rest of her life alone. She deserved a semblance of happiness and perhaps—even at the age of forty-three—a child of her own.

Although the dining room was quickly filling up for the Friday evening supper, Freda walked back slowly to the kitchen. She tried to reconstruct the flow of her morning thoughts about Zushe and herself. There was something delightfully optimistic about them, but the noise of the children wouldn't allow her to recapture them fully. Within minutes, the frenzied activity in the kitchen had flung her back into the demanding world of the hotel.

"You can't work in that dress! Go and change at once!" Rosa, the cook, shouted at her as Freda handed a waiter a tray of twelve soup bowls. But she didn't pay any attention to Rosa and continued working in her bright-green holiday dress.

Freda served supper an hour earlier in order to

give the girls sufficient time to light the Sabbath candles before bedtime. During the supper meal Rosenbloom arrived for his weekend visit. Joseph was waiting for him on the patio.

"Did you bring the BBs?" were the words with which Joseph greeted him.

"Ten packs, as I promised you," Rosenbloom said, then embraced his son. "You see, your father keeps his word." Joseph wriggled out of his grasp and started loading the rifle.

Freda had prepared plates for Asher and Joseph. Although father and son were handed identical plates, Asher ate from Joseph's plate and gave Joseph from his. Joseph wondered why they couldn't eat like everyone else, each one from his own plate.

Zushe was off duty this evening. Wearing a clean, black jacket and a new hat the dentist had brought for him from Montreal only hours earlier, he was busy in the lobby preparing the Sabbath candles. With Freda's help he removed a pile of music books from the piano, then spread a tablecloth over the top. There was only one candelabrum with three holders—not enough for the ten girls who had their mothers' consent to light candles. Freda hurried to the kitchen, returning minutes later with a handful of flat oval potatoes and a sharp little knife.

"Excellent," Zushe said as she began boring holes

into the potatoes. He stuck the candles into the holes, then arrayed the homemade candle holders on either side of the candelabrum.

"Beautiful!" exclaimed Sollie, who was still aching from the cycling ordeal, his arms folded on his abdomen in a gesture of satisfaction.

It was growing dark outside. Zushe lined up the girls and helped them recite the benediction for candle lighting. A number of the women looking on were brought to tears by the sight, by the memories of their own childhoods. Nora also wanted to light candles and Zushe happily obliged. She held the match knowingly beneath the wick until the tiny tongue of flame flared up, then she covered her eyes with her hands, recited the blessing from memory, and wept quietly.

"Is there still time?" Freda called as she strode into the lobby, her hair covered with a long, purple kerchief knotted on her nape.

"You still have two minutes," Zushe answered with a smile.

Freda took a match, struck it hard against the sulphur, breaking it. She took another and broke it also.

"Let me," said Zushe. He calmly lit the match and handed it to her. Their hands overlapped inadvertently in the transfer, both becoming conscious of the touch.

With eyes closed, Freda sang the blessing as her

mother had taught her thirty-five years earlier, intoning each word slowly, with love.

"You have a beautiful voice!" Nora exclaimed in surprise. "Why didn't you tell me all these years? I could have used you in the plays."

There was a hushed silence in the lobby. The sight of the twenty burning candles was an inspiration to everyone. Like a team of wild horses, the flames pulled energetically in the warm breeze blowing in through the patio windows.

Freda was beaming with happiness as she joined the large circle Zushe had formed with the children. He was welcoming the arrival of the Sabbath with the tune traditionally sung when the father returns home from synagogue.

"Peace unto you, ministering angels, messengers of the Most High," he intoned in a clear, lively voice.

The adults recognized the tune, but the children had never heard it. Soon everyone was singing, shuffling along in the circle that now filled the lobby. Even Sollie, who had stood up from the electric seat, was lumbering along, toppling furniture as he went. Quickly exhausted, he fell into a round wicker chair. It took him a few moments to realize that the chair was gradually collapsing under his weight. He got up with the chair attached to him and stood bent over until two men plucked it off him. Nora encouraged him to dance, but Sollie adamantly refused.

When, at last, the crowd dispersed, Zushe went to the patio. A group of cardplayers sat under a mote-filled yellow beam of light. With an oblique nod of greeting, he went down the steps to the deserted front lawn. The mood of euphoria he had experienced at the candle lighting with the girls was waning. Suddenly he envied the cardplayers their laughter. The war had not destroyed them. Certainly they remembered, certainly they mourned, but they had gone on living. They had remarried, started new families. Only he had stopped in the middle of the journey, a living contradiction to all that he pretended to be.

In the peaceful twilight along the beach, these depressing thoughts evaporated into the sultry air and Zushe once again felt the sanctity of the Sabbath. He sensed it in the air, in the sway of the branches, in the calm murmur of the lake. He sauntered through the grounds of the hotel, his black jacket open, his hands behind his back. In the fading remnants of day a sparrow lighted on the beach along the inlet, pecked its beak once into the water, then flew off.

Zushe threw his head back to look up at the trees and the clearing sky. The tree crowns were heavy with foliage and the smell was good. It was all good, he thought, the trees, the grass—knee high in places—and most importantly his presence in the hotel, the culmination of the mission he had set for himself fifteen years ago.

CHAPTER EIGHT

JUST BEFORE BREAKFAST one morning, guests on the patio looked at each other in stunned disbelief as Joseph donned Zushe's tefillin.

Later in the morning, the boy helped the rabbi mount a large mezuzah on the main door of the hotel. News of this latest incursion spread like wildfire through the hotel, but oddly enough no one bothered to make the effort to remove the conspicuous elongated little box on the doorjamb. Some even kissed it with their fingertips when going in or out. An hour after it was mounted, one of the twins got her finger stuck between the door and the frame while attempting to kiss the mezuzah. Dr. Sacks swiftly attended to the minor injury.

After the lunch clean-up, Zushe gathered a group of boys and girls around him in the dining room and related a story.

"Reb Yaakov was his name," Zushe began with a smile tinged by happy memories. "He was in deep old age when I was a child, but whoever saw him once—even for a moment—could never forget him. He used to go in the street with the fringes of his prayer shawl dangling down to his ankles. One day he was stopped by a Polish aristocrat. 'What's that?' demanded the Pole. 'Those are the fringes of my prayer shawl,' responded Reb Yaakov proudly. 'And what's that?' he demanded of the Pole. 'That's my sabre.' 'Well, then this is my sabre,' stated Reb Yaakov as he grabbed hold of the long woollen fringes. 'In that case, let's see whose sabre is stronger!' exclaimed the Pole, and promptly drew the sharp blade out of the sheath. Undaunted, the old man stood his ground. A group of Jews, who were on the scene, came to his rescue. They pleaded with the Pole for mercy, finally convincing him that Reb Yaakov was an old, senile man. After the Pole left, Reb Yaakov expressed his anger to his rescuers. 'Why did you stop the fight?' he shouted at them. 'Here I was about to teach that Gentile a fine lesson and you had to interfere!'"

The audience, now augmented by adults, burst into laughter.

In better times, Beryl would have taken up Zushe's challenge and run the waiter out of the hotel. Now—at all cost—he had to avoid aggravating his ulcers.

But, as Asher Rosenbloom's proxy in the hotel, he felt it his duty to keep an eye on the boy. When Joseph went frog hunting, Beryl's prematurely wrinkled face loosened up with a sense of victory. However, when Joseph sat on the dock gazing reflectively at the lake or the clouds, Beryl was disappointed, and it was Zushe who perceived in the boy a concern for spiritual matters, nodding ever so slightly, a prophetic glint in eyes. In the silences between them, the two men wrestled for Joseph's soul, and in the boy's daily activities they gauged the progress of the battle.

Early one morning, while the guests slept, Zushe walked through the woods to an inlet about a half mile from the hotel. The bright sunlight pierced the canopy of thick, verdant foliage like the tip of a blade. Behind a cluster of evergreens, Zushe got undressed. He took off his shoes and trousers, then the fringed undergarment, which he hung up on a branch. He entered the frigid lake with a firm step. When he was shoulder high in the water, he immersed himself three times. On emerging he took his beard in his hands and squeezed the water out of it. Suddenly, he heard a movement behind him. He finished dressing quickly, then turned towards the source of the sound. It was Freda, standing half-concealed behind bushes.

"I was not watching you," she said apologetically, stepping into the open. Strong emotion showed on her worried face. "I saw you leaving the hotel. I need to talk to you."

He saw that she was embarrassed.

"In the war, men and women walked around half-naked," he said. "No one paid any attention, no one was ashamed."

Zushe picked up the towel, then approached her.

"The guests are giving you trouble," he said with a look that anticipated a problem.

"Many of them want you to leave the hotel!" she blurted out, staring at him with frightened eyes. "I pleaded with them, but they've made up their minds. Some of them are threatening to leave tonight. I don't know what to do."

"I understand," he whispered, nodding slowly as he looked at her with an unhurried gaze. "And you, do you want me to go?"

"No!" she exclaimed, her cheeks aflame. "Of course not! You've helped me so much with the paperwork and in the dining room. Since Gershom died, I've had no one to rely on. I want you to stay. I need you to stay."

"They're only threatening you," he stated confidently.

"Are you sure?" she asked, incredulous. "What should I do then, Zushe?"

"Simply ignore them and go on with your work."

"But what if they do leave?"

"They won't."

"Oh, Zushe, please hold me!" she cried imploringly, releasing herself in his unprepared embrace before he had a chance to extend a detaining hand. "Hold me, I'm so afraid."

He felt the imprint of her body tossing against him with rapid, convulsive sobs.

"Please, sit down," he urged her, taking her hand. He led her to a fallen birch stump and beckoned her to be seated. She complied, but insisted that he sit down beside her.

"I want you to be my partner in the hotel," she said, trying to compose herself. "I've thought it out carefully. I know you have no money to invest, but you'd be investing your time and your knowledge. I couldn't afford to hire someone like you. At the end of the summer whatever the profit will be, we'll share it equally."

Zushe smiled at the proposal, but he saw that his smile agitated her, so he said:

"I'll think about it."

"Please do. I mean what I said."

"I know that."

She drew close to him. From the forest behind them came the scent of wild summer flowers.

CHAPTER NINE

DAY AFTER DAY, Joseph combed the shores of the lake for signs of frog life. Although the lake already abounded with bloated green-white carcasses, he did not grow slack in carrying out his duty. On a number of occasions, he worked the beach near the hotel, in full view of the guests basking in the sun. To his surprise, no one seemed to mind.

One morning he found Zushe standing behind him, observing him in silent disapproval. Turning away from Zushe's gaze, he carried on with his work. When there were no more frogs to be found around the hotel, Joseph drained the water out of a rowboat and pushed off towards more bountiful beaches.

Joseph rowed smoothly through the peaceful lake. On the far shore, the town lay crumpled on a slope, the heavily overcast sky pinned like a circus net on church spires. At an inlet that had teemed with frogs a few days earlier, he was unable to distinguish the frogs from the seaweed. As the sun rose, they gradually emerged from their camouflage. Joseph looked around at the shore to see if anyone was watching him, then raised his rifle. He took careful aim and flipped over the first frog from thirty feet. It lay still for a moment, then crept beneath a scroll of birch, its emerald back glistening moistly.

As the boat drifted towards the shore, dozens of unblinking eyes encircled him. Joseph fired slowly, accurately. A new species of frog came into view, huge, pompous, crouching boldly on exposed rocks and branches. Joseph stared at a frog. A sudden chill went through him on recognizing the features of his father's face as he looked when enraged at his mother. He fired point-blank and hit the frog squarely between the bulging eyes. It went under without a sound and came up floating on its back, twitching convulsively. A fly lighted on its stomach. Joseph shot at the fly.

Gliding in and out of the shadows, Joseph wreaked an awful carnage. He could not stop himself and had he not run out of BBs, he would have gone on until nightfall. Exhausted, he raised the oars and started rowing back to the hotel. Overhead, fat splotches of white cloud drifted lazily across a marble blue sky. Near the hotel dock, a wave slowly lifted the boat up and carried it in.

The weather was exquisite. The guests crowded onto the beach and front lawn. Only the diehard card-players remained on the patio, sweating in the bright sunlight. A dead muskrat was found on the beach in front of the hotel. One of the waiters kicked the carcass into the bushes and there it remained.

The guests mingled leisurely on the front lawn, pausing haphazardly, their faces turned towards the sun, like pedigrees at a cat show. They moved slowly, as though restrained by their own shadows. Children playing in the sand were hardly aware of the silhouettes slithering to and fro over them.

Freda stood on the dock wearing a white apron mottled with bits of hardened dough. She had washed her hair in the morning and now it fluffed intractably over her brow. She bent down, one hand on the loose wooden railing, and called the children in the water to her.

"You have to learn how to swim!" she shouted as a gush of sunrays lit up her face. "Don't waste your time playing ball! Learn how to swim! If my sister had known how to swim, she'd be alive today!"

The children paid no attention to her, quickly resuming their games.

In the deserted lobby after supper the twins were

married. Lea was the groom, Rochl the bride. They stood solemnly holding hands beneath a tablecloth supported by friends. Ten minutes later cries were heard. Lea was clutching her throat. From her few intelligible sounds, it seemed that she had swallowed a bone. This was most peculiar since there were no bones in the food served for supper. But the child insisted there was a bone stuck deep in her throat, and soon the guests were convinced that was the case. Beryl tried to get her to cough it up. When that failed, Freda encouraged her to vomit. She stuck her finger into the child's throat, but Lea bit hard into it, and the poor woman jumped in pain.

"Bone! Bone!" Lea continued to cry hysterically. Freda called for Dr. Sacks, but the dentist was nowhere to be found.

Zushe was on his way to his room when he heard the commotion. He went outside to see what was happening.

"Let me see the bone," he said to the girl.

"What does he know?" someone shouted disparagingly.

"Please open your mouth, Lea," Zushe said gently. "I only want to see how big the bone is." The child relaxed in his presence. As her lips parted, Zushe looked into her mouth, then he nodded with exaggeration to the adults. "It's a big bone all right, but I'm going to take it out in one second."

Zushe put his thumb and forefinger into her mouth, pretended to yank something out, then flung the imaginary bone over the side of the patio.

"It's out!" he told the child, smiling.

She looked at him in surprise and then returned his smile. Suddenly she was feeling much better. Zushe touched her cheek affectionately, then made his way through the crowd that had gathered on the patio.

While the guests were eating supper, Joseph took his rifle and went down to the inlet. He got into a rowboat and pushed off. From the surrounding hills, a murmurous hum flowed across the lake, carrying with it the scent of freshly cut hay. As he rowed past the dock, Joseph saw Zushe approaching from the beach, reciting Psalms from a small open book he held in one hand.

"Come with me," the boy called to him. "You can say Psalms in the boat."

Zushe accepted the invitation. He stepped to the edge of the dock while Joseph backed up the boat. Once Zushe was inside and seated, Joseph pulled away hard from the hotel. In front of them, the horizon smoked purple and orange along feathery bands of cloud.

Joseph guided the boat along the shore towards the town. Rotting, bloated frogs floated upside down among leaves and twigs. Suddenly a huge frog emerged out of the evening camouflage, perched high on a log about fifteen feet away. It was an easy shot, but with Zushe in the boat, he didn't dare attempt it.

Joseph rowed away to an inlet. They got off and stepped to a hillock overlooking the lake. Serrated shadows of tree crowns lay tremulously around their feet.

Zushe tilted back his hat. There was a tuft of hair sticking out from beneath his hat, touching the dip between his eyebrows.

Joseph felt that this was a good time to share the idea he had been thinking about the last few days.

"I want to leave this place. I want to go learn Torah with you in a yeshiva. In Jerusalem. Anywhere. I've decided—I really want to. You'd be saving a Jewish life—isn't that what you're always talking about?"

"You need a normal family life. I can't provide that. I don't know where I'll be the next day."

"You'll marry Freda—everyone in the hotel is talking about it." Zushe smiled. "I'll live with both of you. I won't be a burden. I won't bother you. Then I'll have a normal family like all my friends. I want a mother to take care of me so I don't have to have chips and 7-Up for supper all the time and so I won't have to work Saturday morning in the shipping room so I can buy the chips. God isn't fair with me. Why should I have to suffer because He made a war and then took my mother away from me? I want to go with you to study Torah. Please take me away from here, away from my father. He'll kill me if you don't. I know him. I know him very well."

Zushe also knew him and, seeing the boy's strained expression, unsettled feelings began to stir inside him.

"I need time, Joseph. Let me think about it."

With these words he showed himself to Joseph as wise and cautious and the boy respected him all the more for it.

"One more question, Zushe. Freda told me that you lived in Baranovitch before the war. Did you know my father then? Do you know what happened to my brother and sisters in the ghetto? My father never speaks about it. I really want to know what happened."

"I didn't know your father before the war," Zushe whispered, "and I don't know what happened to the children."

There was something evasive in Zushe's voice but Joseph did not pursue the matter further.

The last Saturday of July, Zushe prayed alone in his room. He had intended to recite the kiddush blessing on wine and to partake of his mid-day Sabbath meal in the dining room, but for some reason the cardplayers had left the patio and were now occupying the dining area. He returned to his room and ate his meal on the makeshift cardboard table. Dr. Sacks had brought wine and a challah from the city the day before and Freda had cooked vegetables for him in a new pot she had not used before. He ate quickly, sitting on a stool near the window.

Zushe left the hotel grounds with a stooped gait, his hat low over his brow. From amid the dispersing clouds, a bright sun toasted his neck and shoulders. He followed the lake road towards the town. In the distance, the railroad station stood deserted, its high dormer reflecting the sunlight. Near the railroad crossing the road climbed sharply. He followed this road to a trail that led into the forest.

The Sabbath laws forbid walking a long distance from a settlement. Zushe mentally measured off the distance from the road and estimated that he could walk for another fifteen minutes. He came to a stagnant green pool. In front of him there was the precipitous face of a mountain, a curtain of rock only yards beyond the pool.

Zushe took the long route around the lake road back to the hotel. Here and there, cows were grazing on the lush green slopes to his left. A damp wind blew, rustling the tree crowns. He stopped and inhaled slowly and deeply, and once again reviewed the details of his plan to kill Asher Rosenbloom.

CHAPTER TEN

THE SHOW in town Thursday evening, July 30, was scheduled to start at seven o'clock. The guests ate quickly and quietly. In a hurry to join the assembly on the front lawn, the waiters had left all the tables for Zushe to clean up.

Beryl stood on the hillock near the roadway and called to the crowd with an expansive arm gesture: "Let's go!"

Sollie was marching frenziedly down the road, determined to get a big head start.

"Stay on the embankment!" Beryl cautioned the guests as they turned out of the hotel grounds.

At last they were all on the road. The motley procession of young and old skirted the lake as the sun cast their long, distorted shadows into the middle of the roadway. Worried that he would be passed and left behind, Sollie kept glancing over his shoulder, his sweat-drenched white shirt glued to his back.

Zushe was the only one left in the hotel. From the deserted patio, he watched the guests walking against the backdrop of the verdant summer landscape. A cool wind was skimming across the lake, filtering through his beard and earlocks. From his vantage point, he saw another scene: the Jews of a shtetl being herded into a forest by SS officers. Zushe closed his eyes and brought his fingers to his pounding forehead. When he opened his eyes, the procession had reached the hill where the road bent sharply to the right. One by one the guests dropped out of view. Zushe imagined a firing squad hiding behind the trees. He shook his head, as if roused from a terrifying dream.

Sollie was still out in front when the guests reached the first bend in the road. Stubbornly refusing to let anyone pass him, he slowed the procession down to a snail's pace. An elderly woman was convinced that they were not going to the town at all, but were being led somewhere else.

"Wait! Wait!" she yelled, but no one paid any attention to her.

Finally Sollie was pushed onto the road and the guests filed quickly past him along the embankment. Freda and Mrs. Steiner walked together holding hands, singing songs. Soon others joined them in a stirring melody of the Jewish partisans.

About a hundred yards from the public beach a circular bandstand with a conical red roof was separated from forty or so rows of freshly painted green benches by a strip of gravel. By the time the hotel guests arrived, most of the seats were taken by the local residents. On either side of the benches, people sat on blankets, bags of food around them. At last everyone was seated, eagerly awaiting the annual show organized by the St. Faustin municipality. Beyond the bandstand the public beach blended into the darkling lake, the Four Leaf Clover Hotel faintly visible in the twilight off to the right.

The bandstand lights were turned on. There was a roll of drums as the curtain was raised and tiny white monkeys came somersaulting across the stage. The crowd looked on with bated breath. Because of the shortage of seats, Joseph sat squeezed between Freda and Sollie. Odours of shmaltz herring and onion wrestled in the air. On stage the master of ceremonies, lustrous from head to foot in a top hat and blue satin suit, tap-danced to the front of the stage. He sang a French song, then pranced backward with exaggerated gestures. A monkey leapt onto his chest, sending him tumbling to the floor, to the rapturous delight of the audience. He bucked to his feet, but as he skipped to the curtain, he accidently stepped on the monkey's tail. There was a squeal of pain. Two young sisters appeared from opposite ends of the stage and burst into song, gesturing as one.

A clown appeared on a one-wheel bicycle and moved jaggedly around the stage. As the audience sat spellbound, Professor Shpitzer leaned over Mrs. Steiner's shoulder to pinch the cheeks of the twins sitting on her lap, smiling proudly at the pink, olive-sized bruise he left on their faces. Mrs. Steiner pushed his arm away with her shoulder, concerned only with the fat, purple grapes she was dropping lovingly, one by one, into the twins' mouths as they gazed raptly at the stage.

"Look, Mother, the monkeys are back!" Lea screamed. "Look, look at the monkeys!"

Alone in the hotel, Zushe worked on Freda's ledgers. He sat in the kitchen with a pile of papers in front of him, but he couldn't concentrate. He was thinking back to the summer of 1939. During those precious months there were moments when he had keenly perceived the wonderful gift of his children and family life and its intoxication had kindled in him belief in God. In those happy summer days the professional world he had striven to conquer was tiny in comparison to the challenge of bringing up children. He was a breadwinner, a father, a husband. There was greatness to be attained amid those appellations—perhaps on a smaller scale than he had aspired to professionally—recognized not in social circles, but in the character of his children and in the happiness of the home.

The sound of the guests returning from the show in town stirred Zushe from his reveries. He closed the ledgers, stood up, and left the hotel through the back door. He walked slowly, throwing his head back from time to time to gaze at the star-filled sky. The sweep of the last twenty years appeared before him like a day. It was only now, as a man in his forties, that he had gained the vantage point to look back on twenty years. A fifth of a century, a significant part of modern history, had vanished before his eyes. In those years a hybrid man had been created, trapped between paralysing grief and Torah logic. Zushe behaved and dressed like an observant Jew, but aside from the skullcap and the fringed undergarment, he wondered if he was really any different than the others in the hotel, if his Torah knowledge really mattered, if indeed it was any match at all for the memories of loss. And the proof that it wasn't he measured in the depth of his need for revenge, a need that now ignored his concern for Joseph, that could rationalize a better life for the boy without his father than with him.

But why was it so, why could he not muster the strength to move on with life? Why was he so mired in the need for revenge? Certainly there had been opportunities to start a new life. Freda, a kind, hard-working lady presented such an opportunity right now. If only he had the will to try. He could work his hours at the hotel, then have time and energy left to study Torah in the evenings. He, a man of many talents, talents that had saved him repeatedly during the war, now had no talent for life. How he had surrendered himself to the past, had focused his existence into an instrument of death—an instrument that he knew could easily turn on him. Could he not let down his guard, his wariness, to surrender his past, to trust again, if not in people, then in God, to whom he supposedly swore allegiance?

And now Joseph had complicated the equation: on the one hand, their warm relationship threatened to sway Zushe from his mission, and on the other, it incited his anger and jealousy that the murderer of his family should be blessed with a healthy, intelligent son while he, the victim, lived in grief and solitude.

CHAPTER ELEVEN

ROSENBLOOM arrived at the hotel earlier than usual the first Friday in August. He brought BBs and a telescope for Joseph's rifle. In his valise, he carried new suits for himself and for Joseph. The boy was playing ping-pong on the back lawn when he noticed his father approaching.

"Here, I have more BBs for you," said Rosenbloom, extending the bag to his son, who took it without a word. "You still have the rifle, don't you?" Joseph nodded silently.

As darkness ushered in the Sabbath, most of the guests were in the lobby, getting ready for the annual children's literary competition. Joseph and Beryl stood on the patio. In front of them the lake lay silent, sprawled out under a clear, purple sky.

"Be calm and pretend you're reading to one person only, to a good friend," Beryl instructed the boy. "Read slowly and carefully. Don't think while you're reading—then you won't get mixed up and the words will come out clearly. Trust in what you've written."

"Don't worry," Joseph replied confidently.

"Your father is inside."

"I know."

"He's so proud of you."

The commotion in the lobby subsided and Nora was heard announcing the first reader. Joseph moved towards the door, but Beryl held him back. He stepped across the patio to the door and turned on the light. He switched it off and on three times in rapid succession. Joseph knew he had deliberately desecrated the Sabbath. With cold anger inflecting his voice, Beryl uttered: "You see, Joseph, today is the Sabbath, but there is no Sabbath and there is no God!"

Nora's oldest daughter was reading when Beryl and Joseph entered the lobby. Her clear, loud voice resounded through the crowded room.

"I'm walking along a deserted, misty street. Shadows of bats crisscross the roadway in front of me. Suddenly I hear the patter of footsteps. I turn around and vaguely discern a human form. It's an old Jew in a prayer shawl. I watch him for a moment, then continue on my way. It's almost as if nothing had happened, but now and again I must glance over my shoulder to be sure I am heading in the right direction."

The girl folded her papers and stood up. Expecting more, the audience momentarily delayed its applause. But finally it came, loud and appreciative. Sollie saw Professor Shpitzer enter the lobby. He stood up with difficulty to offer him the vibrating chair. The twins limped across the stage in unison. Mrs. Steiner reprimanded them, but Lea threatened her angrily: "I'm going to make right here, then I'll be constipated forever!"

Joseph was the last one to read. He sat down on the chair in the middle of the stage, crossed his legs with the confidence of an adult, then began to read.

"The forest calls to me: 'Hurry, Kaplansky, if you want to reach me before the dawn! Hurry!' I struggle through the swampy fields, a faded yellow keyhole in the black sky lighting my way. I was here once before—with you, my Raisele, do you remember? Our laughter danced over these fields and our son played in the high, swaying grass. Where is he, where is our Yankelle? There is no time for mourning—now I must run to the forest. The German patrol is not far behind me. My legs are my friends; they pull me through the swamp. I do not wait for the Messiah to help me. Now the sun peeps over the hills, flooding the fields. At last I am in the forest. The naked, twisted trees scratch me with their frozen fingers. I am safe,

Raisele—another moment to breathe your memory. From beyond a cluster of charred trees—the dead brandishing their arms at God—I hear voices. I step slowly over the spongy earth. In an opening surrounded by trees, a group of Jewish children, dressed in rags, stand huddled around an invisible ark.

"'Children!' I call to them. 'What day is it?' They turn to me, but they do not speak. 'What day is it?' I ask again.

"'Today is Yom Kippur,' whispers the smallest among them, a boy of ten covered in a ripped yellow shawl.

"'Yom Kippur? I did not know.'

"'Come, pray with us.'

"We pray all day in the cold forest. I stand like a chimney over this congregation of children. After sunset they start a fire. I open my sack and hand out the mouldy bread. A piece for you, a piece for you. 'Eat my little brothers, eat.' Later, I ask, 'Children, how is it you survived?'

"'We prayed,' one of them answers.

"'And your families?'

"'We didn't pray enough,' replies another.

"The night sweeps darkness over our little camp. One by one the children fall asleep. But I cannot sleep. I must find food for them. A last backward glance and I slip away. I wander all night in search of a farmhouse, deceived by a flirtatious moon. Daylight finds me near a clearing. I push my way through the bushes. Ah, my little friends, asleep just as I had left them.

"'Time to get up,' I call to them. No one stirs. I bend down to shake one of them—the fleshless arm replies with a heavy plea. And so the others. I do not understand. As I search their bodies for a clue, I feel a sudden choking. No! This cannot be! This is not the blood of Jewish children!"

Joseph paused reflectively. He looked up at the deeply moved audience, then whispered in a low, cracking voice: "But was not yesterday Yom Kippur?"

Spontaneous, tearful applause accompanied Joseph as he strode across the stage towards Beryl, who embraced him ecstatically.

"You're a writer!" Beryl affirmed. "Yes, you're a writer in the old tradition!"

Zushe happened to be standing nearby. Beryl turned a spiteful, mocking gaze upon him, as if to exclaim: "He's one of us! Him you will never have!"

Joseph, too, was excited, and not even Zushe's steadfast eyes could lessen the high emotion of the moment. Rosenbloom approached to embrace his son. Blushing, eyes lowered, the boy submitted for a moment, then broke free from the hold and ran out.

That night in their room, Asher took out a roll of bills from his pocket and peeled off a ten-dollar bill.

He handed it to Joseph who was getting ready for bed. The boy left it on the bed where his father had dropped it.

"It's a present for you. You did well tonight. Beryl and I are very proud of you. You see, you don't need that stinking rabbi to help you succeed."

"He hasn't done me any harm," Joseph answered. "He's really a kind person. I've seen him help many people in the hotel."

"Always with a calculation. I know his type better than you. And now he's tricked you into putting on tefillin. What's his business, anyhow?"

"He hasn't tricked me. I like putting on tefillin. I really do."

"A child doesn't know what he likes or doesn't like."

"I'm not a child, and I do know what I want."

Joseph saw that his father was growing angry. He put on his slippers, then moved to the door.

"I have to go to the bathroom," he said, excusing himself.

Once in the corridor, he burst into tears.

CHAPTER TWELVE

ONLY ZUSHE was able to step in and out of the desultory conversations of the two elderly chessplayers. By dint of his self-confidence and intelligence he had been co-opted into their exclusive club. From time to time he moved a piece on behalf of one of the players and no one seemed to mind. Mr. Dimant chattered endlessly about European history and literature while Professor Shpitzer responded with smatterings of mathematics and Greek philosophy. The chessplayers regarded Zushe as an impartial judge of their continuing discussions, nodding gratefully whenever he made a comment, as though he had finally cleared up some thorny point of contention between them. The two-way dialogue had been enlarged, but occasionally Zushe guided it subtly in a direction neither of the chessplayers had intended.

One evening Zushe returned from a walk to find Professor Shpitzer and Mr. Dimant on the patio in a boring endgame that had been going on for many hours. Mr. Dimant was scratching his forehead as he and a group of sleepy onlookers listened to Professor Shpitzer.

"He was a Jew all along," Professor Shpitzer affirmed. "You have to understand what was happening then. Tens of thousands of Jews were joining up with him."

"Who are you talking about?" Mr. Dimant asked absently.

"Yeshu."

"Jesus?"

"Who else?"

"Peter knew he had to stop the defections from the faith, so he joined Yeshu's followers. His plan was to write material for them that was so extreme it would make traditional Jews return to the fold. For example, he said that circumcision was unnecessary, that the laws for kosher food were senseless, and so on and so on. To turn this far away from traditional Judaism, most of Yeshu's followers weren't prepared, and in fact many of them did return to Judaism. But then Peter was in a dilemma: he had written such things which made it impossible for him to return to the Jewish community. He knew the Jews would never believe his true motives, so he removed himself from them and lived his remaining years in a cave studying Torah."

"Checkmate," whispered Mr. Dimant.

Professor Shpitzer examined the board carefully and saw that it was indeed so. Smiling, he began to arrange the pieces for another game.

Joseph appeared on the patio in his pyjamas and slippers. Zushe greeted him with a smile. He sat down next to the professor, who gave him a pat on the back. Professor Shpitzer began talking about Einstein's famous equation.

"When you think about it, Dimant, it's really quite extraordinary! Imagine, energy is equal to mass."

"I weigh a hundred and fifty-two pounds in my underwear," said Mr. Dimant. "So how much energy does that make?"

"You'd have to be travelling at the speed of light—that's the 'c' in the equation," retorted the professor with a note of impatience.

"So how do I do that?"

"Why would you want to do that? You'd disintegrate in a second!"

"I see," muttered Mr. Dimant.

"What an equation!" the professor sighed. "How did he think of it? $E=mc^2$!"

"There's another interesting equation," observed Zushe, immediately drawing everyone's attention.

"It's an equation of life and it says: yes is equal to no."

"Yes is equal to no?" Professor Shpitzer asked quizzically, crinkling up his nose, bestirring himself from the numbness of the chronic chess games. "That certainly is surprising, but how is it possible?"

"Why it's very easy to understand, Professor Shpitzer," replied Zushe, maintaining an interested gaze on the board. "Consider a man who's very ill, God forbid. Does he worry about his business or his wealth? If you told him that his business had gone bankrupt, it wouldn't bother him in the slightest. Or, if he was informed that he had won a million dollars, he wouldn't celebrate. For a critically sick man, anything to do with the physical world has one value: for him, yes is exactly the same as no."

"I suppose you have a point," conceded Mr. Dimant as his fingers hovered above a pawn.

"Because his life hangs on a hair, the sick man knows the formula yes equals no," Zushe went on in his calm, unhurried voice. "But in truth, the life of every man constantly hangs on a hair. Only he's not aware of it. God gives us life every second anew. From that perspective, the equation yes is equal to no applies to everyone and all the time. It's a true equation of life."

"Maybe, maybe," mumbled Professor Shpitzer abstractedly. About an hour later, Zushe observed obscurely: "We, the firemen of time, await the fire."

For fifteen minutes the remark went unanswered. Joseph, who stood nearby, was baffled by the statement. At length, Professor Shpitzer asked, "Who are the firemen?"

"The Jews," Zushe said with feigned indifference.

Another fifteen minutes went by in silence.

"And what's the fire?" asked Mr. Dimant.

"The conflagration just before the coming of the Messiah," Zushe replied nonchalantly, as though the subject he had brought up was the last thing on his mind.

"Yes, we're all waiting for the Messiah," Professor Shpitzer affirmed, contemplating the board. "But when will he come? When? We've been waiting for two thousand years."

"Soon, very soon," Zushe promised in a whisper.

It had rained Saturday in the late afternoon but now the flotilla of clouds was dispersing from the evening stage. A white, silt-like dew covered the front lawn. The air was cool and fresh and the guests, dressed in their finest, inhaled deeply, their contented faces swelling with each breath.

In the gathering twilight the yellow light over the patio awning gouged out a turbid sphere of dust and moths. Zushe met Freda in the lobby. She was wearing a long-sleeved, blue dress, her hair combed attractively to one side. He paused to greet her, but realized immediately that she was serving the card-players. Nodding slightly, he stepped away.

He walked past the inlet to the road, the inner tension pulsing within him, along the well-established tributaries of pain. But it was different now; in his heart he held the hope that very soon he would be able to move on with his life. He guarded this almost palpable sensation of final liberation, marvelling at how far God had brought him in his quest.

A puddle on the road caught the light of a distant lamp, reflecting Zushe's shadow. He strained to see his face, but could not discern the features of a human. He followed the road up around the back lawn of the hotel, his head bent, his hands behind his back. On his left, the high poplars surrounding the hotel stood like lonely sentinels against the dark backdrop of the lake.

Zushe entered the back lawn along a narrow pathway. The shrubbery thickened on both sides as he walked on. The war and the long years of searching had taught him to be wary. Like a cat in unfamiliar surroundings, he stepped cautiously down the path, one fist clenched instinctively at his side. Suddenly, there was a rustling in front of him. Asher Rosenbloom stood alone near a bench. He was wearing a suit and a tie and a black beret, angled sharply to a side.

"Good *Shabbes*," Zushe said, standing slightly

stooped in the dim light of a lamp about twenty feet away. The patch of light on the grass was wedged apart by Zushe's advancing shadow.

"It's not easy bringing up a boy without a mother," Rosenbloom began in an agitated voice, standing erectly between two evergreens. "I suppose you don't mean him any harm, but most of us simply can't come to terms with your God. You have, but we can't. That, too, must be respected by you. I don't want Joseph to wear a skullcap. It proves nothing. What matters is what's in your heart." Zushe stared at him with fixed eyes. "My son has to return to the city. He's all I have left in this world. He must succeed in life. I don't want him to be a labourer like his father, in a dirty business. He'll be a professional, an engineer, a doctor. There's a retired teacher in the city who is going to prepare him for algebra. That's why I want him to come back with me. But he doesn't want to leave the hotel because of you. I want you to tell him to listen to his father."

Zushe nodded compehendingly, then remarked with surprise, "But isn't there a polio epidemic in the city?"

"It's been over for weeks."

"From what little I know, these things take a long time to be completely over. Might not the boy be safer here in the fresh air than in the city? And as for the algebra, perhaps the teacher could send the work here with you? Then I could tutor him. I know the subject well. I was a teacher before the war."

"It's more than the polio."

"Yes, of course, it's your fear of Torah. But is that a real fear, Asher? Surely you attended yeshiva yourself as a child."

"I don't want to hear any more!" he interrupted with anger, nodded snappily, as if in a salute, turned, and walked away.

"Girls! Girls!" Mrs. Steiner's voice was heard. "I have raisins for you! Raisins!"

"We don't want raisins!" they shouted back.

As she chased them around the beach, Mrs. Steiner stumbled on a hole and lost most of the raisins she had been holding in her hand. She regained her balance and ran after the twins, her thumb and forefinger together, with the mistaken sensation that there was a raisin clasped between them.

During lunch Mrs.Weinberg cleared her throat and stood up. The tall, imperious-looking woman wore a white fur cap, unaware that strawberry jam was smeared across one side. Dusty sunbeams slanting through the windows pointed her shadow towards the kitchen door.

"When the SS came to our house, the children were lined up, but my son's left shoe was not on," she said tremulously. "There was a big knot on one side and I couldn't tie up the ends, so he had to walk with one shoe flopping up and down. That's all I wanted to tell you."

She sat down and gazed blankly at the windows. Shortly afterwards, there was a second unexpected reminiscence—this time from Nora. The director of entertainment stood up on a chair to address the guests.

"I used to buy the eggs for our family when I was a little girl. My mother—may she rest in peace—would send me to a farmer who lived on the outskirts of our shtetl. One day she found an egg with a double yoke. As soon as she saw this, she put money into my pocket and sent me back to the farmer: 'Hurry up, he made a mistake, we didn't pay him enough money.'"

Nora stepped slowly down from the chair.

Suddenly the dentist, who had never seen a German soldier in his life, felt obliged to address the guests. With a cup of coffee in his left hand, he stood up and began to speak in a broken, drawling Yiddish.

"When I was a boy I wanted to be a doctor, but when I applied to medical school at McGill University, they didn't accept me because I was a Jew—I mean, because I am a Jew. So I had to become a dentist."

"So what's wrong with a dentist?" someone called out. "A dentist is a doctor also. He's a doctor and a dentist—two professions."

"Thank you, thank you," Dr. Sacks muttered tearfully, deeply moved, feeling that he was one of them. Sollie left his dessert, stepped up to him, and patted him on the back in a display of solidarity. Dr. Sacks nodded his gratitude to the guests and sat down to eat the ice cream that had long melted.

CHAPTER THIRTEEN

A BRIGHT WARM SUN shone on the hotel grounds Sunday in the late afternoon. For once the cardplayers showed more interest in their vacations than in poker. Beryl loosened the grip on his cards, unbuttoned his shirt, and grinned at his neighbours, relaxed. While the cards were being shuffled, he slapped his palm down on the table; it was a signal for the twins to run up to him and place their hands on top of his until a six-step staircase took shape. Then Beryl slipped his bottom hand out and the edifice collapsed. The game was over and the twins shuffled despondently to the patio railing, where they stood in tense readiness, waiting for another turn. Once Beryl surprised them and slapped the table before they had returned to their posts and they came running back for a repeat performance, laughing so loudly Shloymeh had to block his ears.

Just before supper, the children queued up on the patio to have their eyesight checked. The dentist had prepared a chart. He mounted it on the railing near the card tables, then paced off four yards towards the children.

"Okay, you're first, Gerald," said Dr. Sacks. "Cover your left eye with your hand."

"E-F-P-T-Z-O-Z-L-D-E-D-P-C-F-D . . . " Gerald read quietly.

"Perfect!" the dentist exclaimed.

"He's a genius!" Gerald's mother cried with elation, hugging her son.

A crowd soon gathered at the scene, and after each successful recital, there was a burst of applause.

Mrs. Steiner wanted the twins checked.

"They're too young," asserted Dr. Sacks. "They don't even know the ABC."

"Never mind," Mrs. Steiner insisted, jostling Lea into the front of the line. "Read the letters!" she ordered. Lea covered her left eye and rattled off her favourite letter: "P-P-P. . . ."

On the front lawn, older children were roasting marshmallows over a small bonfire. Joseph stood near the dock, rifle in hand, when his father approached in full stride.

"Pack your things, you're going home with me in an hour!"

The command took the boy by surprise.

"Why?" he asked, avoiding his father's burning glare.

"The polio epidemic is over. There's no reason to stay any longer."

Joseph did not believe him.

"I was supposed to stay the whole summer! There are still three weeks left!" he shouted.

Suddenly Rosenbloom's hand lashed out and caught the boy hard across the face. Joseph burst into tears.

"You're screaming at your father!" he yelled as a crowd gathered around them. Then he struck the boy again across the shoulder, sending him to his knees. Beryl ran to the scene and tried to restrain the enraged Asher.

"Enough, enough. He's only a boy. Leave him, leave him."

"What I've lived through and he could shout at me!" Rosenbloom spluttered, his fists clenched.

Joseph stood up. He searched for Zushe among the gaping faces, but could not find him. Gerald was standing beside him, holding his rifle. The crippled boy extended his free hand to help Joseph up. Together they hobbled away towards the patio.

Joseph did not go to the dining room for supper. While the others ate he left the hotel grounds. He held his rifle in one hand and a Dostoyevsky novel in the other. As he walked hurriedly down the road girdling the lake, the wind-swept rain sprayed his face and inspired him to move faster. He followed a path into the forest where it became a narrow trail, winding through fir and birch. Overhead the canopy of tree crowns diffused the turbid sunlight. A blue ribbon of a stream appeared from the shrubbery, reflecting fragments of a dull sky. Joseph emerged from the forest on a mountain ridge. On a clear day he could have seen across the valley to the other side, but today a heavy mist blotted out wide areas.

He found a patch of dry grass in a clump of pines, made himself comfortable against a trunk, and began reading, holding the book upright so it would not get wet in the drizzle. He read ten pages, then fell asleep.

When he awoke, he did not know whether the twilight meant the approach of night or day. Soaked through and through, he did not have the strength or the desire to move.

Hours later he heard his name being called from the distance.

"Joseph. Joseph."

On recognizing Zushe's voice, he bolted to his feet.

"I'm here, here," he answered hoarsely, water pouring down his face.

There was a movement among the trees, then Zushe appeared, drenched from head to foot.

"What are you doing here?" Joseph asked in bewilderment.

"It's after eight o'clock—you've been gone for hours. Everyone in the hotel is looking for you."

"How did you know where I was?"

"Gerald told me. He said you often go to featherland. Isn't that what this place is called? Are you all right?"

"Yes, of course," the boy replied, unaware that his lips were trembling.

Zushe had brought an apple with him. He handed it to Joseph and beckoned him to eat. The boy bit off a chunk, but didn't bother chewing it. Zushe placed the palm of his hand on the boy's forehead. He felt warm.

"Can you walk?" Zushe asked with concern.

Joseph took a step and stumbled forward. As they began walking, he realized that he had left his rifle behind. He alluded to it with a sidelong glance and Zushe went to get it while Joseph leaned against a tree. Once on the way, the boy began mumbling.

"My father won't let me talk to you. He wants to take me back to Montreal. I hate him! He tortures me at home! He puts a razor blade to his throat, then locks himself in the cellar! I knock on the door for hours, begging him not to kill himself. Then he finally comes out and pretends that nothing happened. He expects me to forget, but I can't! He tortured my mother like that until she died. Then he says I laughed at her deathbed. It's a lie! He's a torturer. He worked in the NKVD and he's proud of it too!"

The boy thought about an incident that would bring his words home to Zushe. Joseph's face clouded, then tears welled up in his eyes.

"Was it my fault I didn't win a scholarship to high school? For weeks he tortured me for that! Why did Leibelle win a scholarship and not me! He asked me that a thousand times! I had to give him an answer, but I didn't have any answer to give. I don't know why Leibelle won and I didn't. I couldn't answer, so I just kept quiet. Then he got angry with me for not talking to him, and he lay down on the kitchen floor and pretended to be dead. I shook him and shook him, but he's an excellent actor and I wasn't sure if he was dead or alive. It's not my fault he lost his family in the war! I didn't kill them! Why should I have to suffer because Hitler killed them?"

Joseph's unburdening sobs quickened and he could no longer speak. Zushe drew him into his embrace and stroked his head tenderly.

"I hate him!" Joseph cried out from the depths of his heart.

"All right, all right," Zushe whispered consolingly.

It was still raining hard and the boy was running a fever. Zushe tried to urge him on, but he could hardly walk.

"I'm thirsty," Joseph murmured.

"There's a stream not far from here."

They walked slowly along a swampy path until they reached the stream. Zushe bent down to scoop up a handful of water. He brought it to Joseph's lips, then wiped the boy's cheeks and brow with his wet hand.

"I can't walk any more," Joseph pleaded.

"We'll rest a little while here."

Zushe helped him sit down under a thick evergreen near the stream. He stepped away, returning a few minutes later with a handful of dry pine needles. The rain had stopped but water was dripping from his beard as he bent down to search for stones in the stream. At last he found what he was looking for. He took two flat stones and struck them repeatedly against each other over the little heap of needles. Sparks flew out in all directions. Finally one struck the needles and kindled a fire. Zushe protected the tiny flame with his hands, adding twigs as it grew bigger and bigger. Soon a warm, crackling fire had dispelled the twilight around them.

"A flintstone lies for years in water, but the fire it contains inside is never lost," Zushe said, displaying the stones to Joseph. "And it's the same with a Jew.

Every Jew has a godly fire within him. It's there even though he can't see it. With a little effort, it can be brought into the open."

"You know, I can't figure you out," Joseph said. "You wear a skullcap, you talk about God and all that stuff, but there's something very strange about you. I can't explain it exactly." Zushe laughed, but it didn't allay the boy's suspicion. "Why did you come to the hotel? It doesn't make sense. You don't belong here. The food isn't kosher, there's no synagogue, and the guests don't like you. Why do you stay? There's something very odd in all this. You can tell me, Zushe. I'll keep your secret."

With unblinking eyes, Zushe gazed into the fire, humming a tune in a low, ardent voice.

"What do you want to be when you'll grow up?" he asked, changing the direction of the conversation.

"A medical scientist. When my mother died of cancer, I made a vow I'd find a cure for it. But I also want to be a writer in my spare time."

"The black smell of earth," Zushe lilted poetically. "Can a smell be black?"

"Of course it can!" Joseph averred.

"Then you'll certainly be a writer!" Zushe said, smiling at the boy.

There was a momentary silence, then Joseph reverted to his thoughts about Zushe.

"You believe in God, yet you're really no different

than the guests in the hotel. You're broken just like the others but no one can see it."

These words caught Zushe off guard. It was something he would have said about himself, but to hear it from a boy of thirteen stung him.

"There's nothing more whole than a broken heart," he answered. He searched the ground around their feet. Turning around, he picked up a long twig that lay on the grass behind them and bent it into a circle with both hands.

"You see, Joseph, the twig has been changed forever—it has been broken as a twig—but now it has become a complete circle."

The answer was painful to Joseph, but it was an answer he could understand.

"You're a very strange person," Joseph said.

"And there's something very strange about you," Zushe replied with a wry smile. "How many boys go about killing frogs day after day?"

Joseph did not answer.

Zushe stood up and helped Joseph to his feet. The boy tried to walk, but he couldn't. Zushe lifted him up and carried him through the forest. Joseph fell asleep with his arm around Zushe's neck.

Rosenbloom was supposed to have left for Montreal an hour ago. Now he was pacing the lamp-lit patio, cursing his son for the delay. When Zushe staggered onto the hotel grounds carrying Joseph in his arms, Asher burst into tears.

"He has fever," Zushe said, exhausted, as Freda approached him on the run, wringing her hands.

The commotion awakened Joseph. Groggy-eyed, he stared at his weeping father. Asher hugged his son who was too weak to resist and, with his mouth wide open, kissed him repeatedly, clumsily, on the head and on the face. At length he released the boy. He took him by the hand and led him towards the patio steps.

After lunch the next day, Zushe approached Joseph on the front lawn.

"How are you feeling?" he asked with a smile.

"Much better—no more fever."

"Thank God. Are you up to a trip, Joseph?"

"Yes, of course. Where?"

"I'm taking the noon train to St. Agathe."

"We'll have to run to the station then."

"God gave us legs, didn't He?"

"Why are we going?" Joseph queried as they ran down the road together.

"Freda has agreed to use kosher meat. There's a slaughterhouse there."

They followed the road halfway around the lake, arriving at the station only minutes before the train. Once inside, they sat down in the back of the last car.

Huge boulders studded the hills along the embankment as the train wound its way slowly through the mountains. Some bore messages smeared in paint. One in particular caught Zushe's eye: Phillipe et Loũise—juillet 1943.

Where was I in July 1943? he asked himself ruefully, staring into the distance.

"What are you thinking about?" Joseph stirred him from his reveries.

"Nothing, nothing," he replied evasively.

"Do you really believe that the Messiah will ever come?" the boy asked, thinking about a conversation he had with Zushe the previous week.

"If we really want him to come, he'll come."

"But of course we want him to come," Joseph responded with a puzzled look.

"It's easy to say that," Zushe whispered with a sigh. "There was once a king," he began in a storytelling voice as the train turned between thickly foliaged hills. "He had a son who didn't behave well, so the king sent him to the house of a certain peasant, who was given the job of improving the character of the king's precious, only son. Some time went by and the king came to visit his son. There was improvement in the son's character, but he was still far from being the kind of person the king wanted him to be. The son wanted to go home, but the king saw that he wasn't ready, so he ordered the peasant to continue working with him. Another few months went by and the king came to visit again. When he entered the peasant's house, he found his son crying. 'Why are you crying?' he asked. The son answered, 'Father, please tell the peasant not to beat me so much.' When the king heard these words, he burst into tears."

Zushe paused, nodding thoughtfully while he waited for Joseph to grasp the meaning of the story.

"Do you understand, Joseph? The king was hoping that his son would want to go home, but the son had become so accustomed to the hardships at the peasant's house that all he cared about was the improvement of his physical conditions. If only his son had said, 'Take me home, Father,' the king would have done it happily. And it's the same with the Jews now. We've suffered so much that all we want is to have a little more money, a television, even a car. We've forgotten the main thing, just like the king's son; we've forgotten to ask God to take us home. We have only to ask with a sincere heart and He'll do it. He wants to do it. He knows how much we've suffered, and He's only waiting for us to ask."

It was a hot, humid day and the streets of St. Agathe were crowded with colourfully clad pedestrians. Balloons festooned the streets and from the public beach the clamour of children's voices sounded like a traffic jam.

They walked to the slaughterhouse on the outskirts of the town, a drab industrial building surrounded by an unpaved parking lot. Zushe seemed to know his way around the place. He led Joseph through a dark corridor between pens packed with livestock. A pungent, yellow steam drifted through the plant, pushed along by the sounds of men shouting in French.

They entered the slaughtering area through a side door. Along high scaffolds cows dangled upside down, hanging by one leg, in various stages of process. Now and then the slowly swinging carcasses grazed each other and moved apart. Joseph watched with gaping eyes as a man in a grey uniform, carrying a rifle, approached a pen where a cow's head was sticking out through a hole in a metal door. He pressed the barrel to the middle of the forehead and fired. As the side door of the metal pen was raised, the animal slumped out, crashing to the cement floor, blood gushing from the mouth and nostrils. A steel hook was attached to the left hoof and the animal hoisted high onto the assembly line, its free leg dangling sideways, kicking spasmodically upward. On narrow landings amid the scaffolds, tattooed men with cigarettes in their mouths sharpened their knives.

Zushe spoke to a man about transferring the meat to the hotel once he would be through with his work. Everything was arranged. Zushe walked to the slaughtering pen with Joseph behind him. A calf had been prepared, its neck stretched up to the cavernous room.

He drew the ritual slaughtering knife out of his jacket pocket, then carefully tested the blade on the fingernail of his thumb. Although he had done it many times before, he now felt unsure of himself. He raised the blade slowly to the underside of the nape and, with one brisk movement of the wrist, it was over. Blood gushed to the floor as the calf's head fell back against the door of the pen, it's eyes ogling upward.

Zushe felt a sudden weakness in his knees. He stepped to Joseph, embraced him with both arms, the dripping knife in his trembling right hand.

CHAPTER FOURTEEN

THE FOLLOWING MORNING, Beryl excused himself from a poker game and left the hotel. He walked slowly into the forest. The lace of his right shoe was undone, but he didn't bother trying to tie it. He was thinking about the war, how looking back, one saw only suffering on the scale of millions. But he wondered about men like him, men who had developed stomach ulcers. Where on the scale of suffering was the stomach pain he had first experienced in the box cars? Where was the anguish of infants being stifled into silence, the agonizing words between man and wife as they were being separated forever? Where were those little things now, the seemingly insignificant details adhering to the larger tragedies, to the vast numbers of dead? For him, they had never lost their significance.

Indeed, over the years, they had become more intense, developing into vicious incurable ulcers, slowly devouring him from within and reducing the quality of his life to the point where he wondered if it was worth living.

He returned to the hotel just as Dr. Sacks drove into the driveway. In the back seat he had a life-sized, brightly coloured anatomical drawing of the digestive tract.

"Beryl, you must try to understand the anatomy of the colon!" he asserted excitedly once they were in the lobby. "Otherwise, I don't know if I can help you. It's really quite simple. Here, you see, the pipe goes up the right side of the abdomen to the corner there, then arcs down across the front, and finally descends along the left side to you-know-what. Air is light, so it floats up and gets stuck in that corner. That's where your pain is coming from. If you'll lie down on your stomach with your left side turned upward slightly, the air trapped in the corner should slip into the transversal section, and then down into you-know-what and the gas will come out. I want you to try that after supper."

"Immediately after supper?" Beryl asked in surprise.

"You should wait the usual forty-five minutes to let the food get through the duodenum."

"That's what I meant."

"Yes, of course. And when you do that, listen carefully to your colon. If you hear it pulsing, you'll know it's working properly."

"Thank you, thank you," Beryl whispered gratefully.

Dr. Sacks hung the drawing up on the lobby wall over the piano, then stepped back and gazed at it with pride and genuine amazement.

It poured the rest of the day. After supper, the guests gathered in the lobby. Along the back wall, two poker games were in progress. Joseph sat nearby reading a book Zushe had given him. Directly in front of him, Professor Shpitzer and Mr. Dimant were playing what was to be the last game of the day. It was the professor's turn to move, but he was in no hurry. Gerald sat on his accordion case reading a comic book. Annoyed by the youth's inability to speak a word of Yiddish, the professor admonished him.

"The worst Frenchman can speak French, so why can't you speak Yiddish?" Fondling his mane, his lips damp and curled outward, he shook his head in utter incomprehension.

Gerald stood up and hobbled away in a huff.

"You shouldn't embarrass him," reproved Freda, who had just arrived with a tray of cookies. "It's not becoming of a professor."

The professor nodded, but it wasn't clear if he

agreed with her or not. In a particularly loquacious mood this evening, he tugged absently on a tuft of hair over his left ear.

"If I were God, I never would have allowed Hitler to exist," he proposed.

"If I were God, there would be no such thing as illness," declared Mr. Dimant.

"If I were God, I would bring back to life every one of the six million," opined Freda, nodding proudly.

The guests who had gathered around the chess-players wholeheartedly approved of Freda's noble sentiment. One after the other, they proclaimed what they would do if they were God. Standing nearby with a broom in hand, Zushe smiled sadly as he listened to the suggestions. The rim of his hat, high over his brow, gave wide sweep to his wrinkled forehead.

When, at last, there was a moment of silence, Zushe said quietly, "If I were God, I would leave everything exactly the way it is."

The statement astounded the listeners. Professor Shpitzer blinked his eyes and shook his head as though a bucket of cold water had been poured on him.

But Joseph smiled; Zushe had said exactly what he had expected him to say.

"We don't know enough Torah to be good," suggested Mr. Dimant, as though it somehow explained Zushe's statement.

"If we conducted ourselves in accordance with the little we do know, we'd all be saints," Zushe said in a more complaisant voice.

"He's right," stated Freda. "Everyone knows you're not allowed to kill, still everyone goes around murdering each other."

"True, true," Mr. Dimant concurred as he inadvertently moved a pawn into danger.

Professor Shpitzer was proud of the fact that he was a Reform-minded Jew. In a discussion with him a few days ago, Zushe had expressed his clear annoyance with the professor's ideas. Tonight he decided to set matters straight.

When Mr. Dimant said to Zushe, "Please make my move for me," Zushe moved the castle diagonally.

"You can't do that!" Professor Shpitzer objected vehemently.

"Oh, why not?" asked Zushe, feigning a surprised look on his handsome, smiling face.

"What do you mean? Because it's not chess, that's why!"

"Oh?" Zushe responded. "Then I suppose you're right. But isn't it the same with your Reform Judaism? You've changed the rules of Judaism, but insist on calling it just that."

The professor made no attempt to refute Zushe's

argument. With eyes fixed on the board, he continued to play, but his concentration was not what it usually was and he quickly lost the game to Mr. Dimant.

Suddenly, the lights went out. The cardplayers grumbled irritably, clutching their money in the twilight. Professor Shpitzer and Mr. Dimant continued their chess game as though nothing had happened. For a while the guests milled about in the dusky light, then matches were lit up, exposing the extent of night's deep invasion.

The guests crowded anxiously into the lobby. Here and there, the glow of a cigarette lit up a worried face. Finally candles were found and lit.

Shortly after the electricity had returned, a car drove into the driveway. Asher Rosenbloom had come up from the city. Gerald was standing near the patio windows when he saw him get out of the car.

"Joseph!" he yelled. "Your father is coming."

The youth dropped the book he was reading as his heart leapt with fear. Beryl went out to greet Asher on the patio. After exchanging a few words, they entered the lobby together. Asher seemed to be in a good mood, but no one knew why he had come in the middle of the week.

Late that evening, after he had mopped the dining-room floor, Zushe sat alone working on the hotel ledgers. Suddenly Asher appeared in the doorway. Zushe heard him enter and stood up to face him.

"You don't remember me, do you?" he asked, gazing sternly at Asher. "I lived at Twenty-four Kosyakin Street." Rosenbloom's eyes narrowed as he tried to recognize Zushe. "There was a large oak in front of our house. The Polish Architecture School was across the street. Who didn't know Asher Rosenbloom, the wealthy landowner? You knew me as George Katznelson. I didn't have a beard then and I didn't wear a skullcap."

"I don't recognize you," Rosenbloom stammered, half closing one eye behind the small round glasses. "I don't know who you are."

"Your wife's name was Henye Tannenhouse," Zushe said. "But of course you remember me—we were in the cellar together with the survivors after the first *Aktion*."

"I don't remember a Katznelson family in the ghetto," Asher said, shaking his head in confirmation. "I don't know what cellar you're talking about. We escaped before the transports began."

"No, Asher, your memory must be deserting you," Zushe replied. "You remained in the cellar with your wife and children. I was there with you."

Zushe took off his glasses, coiled up his beard, and removed his skullcap. He showed himself as a version of the young high school teacher he had once been.

Asher seemed to recognize him, but he was not ready to admit more than a vague recollection.

"Your family?" Asher inquired.

"Someone betrayed them in the cellar." Asher nodded sympathetically. "Three men went out in search of food. I was one of them. When we returned the following night, there was no one in the cellar. One of those who had stayed behind had informed the SS."

"There were a hundred people in the cellar," Asher replied, trying to conceal his obvious agitation. "I don't remember who was there and who wasn't there. I know men did anything to save their skins. It was part of the war. It was unavoidable. Yes—they came and took us to the small square and from there we were led to the ghetto around Krisnianski Square. Two days later the second transports began."

"And your family?" Zushe asked, stepping back from the brink of accusation.

"My wife survived with me—not my children. Joseph was born after the war. My wife died of cancer six months ago. And you—did anyone survive?"

"No one."

Asher glanced anxiously at him, then said, "Who didn't lose relatives?" He drew an envelope out of his pocket and offered it to Zushe. "Here's a thousand dollars cash. Take it—it's for you. It's all my savings.

Take it and leave the hotel. Then Joseph will come back with me to the city."

"I don't need your money," Zushe retorted firmly.

"Then tell him to go home with me. He's been here more than a month. It's enough. The polio epidemic is over in the city."

As Zushe looked away to resume his work, Rosenbloom grabbed his sleeve.

"I've tried to be reasonable with you, but you don't want to understand." Gritting his teeth, Asher warned, "If you don't let him come back with me, I'll have to kill you."

Zushe stood his ground, then whispered, "I will not be the first Jew you killed."

He had uttered these words with such certainty that Asher stood dumbfounded in the silence between them.

Zushe had exposed himself, lost the advantage of surprise. He was now in danger but it did not matter to him.

"Good evening," Zushe said, affecting a polite nod, and stepped away, satisfied that he had accomplished what he had intended in this the first skirmish to wrest Asher's confession before killing him.

Rosenbloom remained standing with his hands in his pockets lumped into fists.

CHAPTER FIFTEEN

JOSEPH saw Zushe not only as a man of uncompromising faith. In the rabbi's outlook on life, there seemed to be room for other ideas, an openness that appealed to Joseph. Nothing convinced him more of this than an incident that occurred in mid-August, the evening of Tisha B'av, the fast day commemorating the destruction of the Temple in Jerusalem two thousand years ago.

As the sun was setting, Zushe sat down on the floor of the lobby to eat a hard-boiled egg which he dipped in ashes. He wore slippers and the ragged clothes with which he first appeared at the hotel. When asked what he was doing, he answered that Tisha B'av was about to begin, then explained the meaning of the day.

Beryl appeared on the scene. He had been having

severe abdominal pain all day and was in a bad mood.

"I remember Tisha B'av very well," he said. "It was the day of the first slaughter in our shtetl. At one o'clock, when the *Aktion* was completed, I overheard an SS officer surveying the scene of destruction and the surviving Jews. "So many *Juden* are still alive?" he sighed with frustration. A mother and two children stood nearby dazed. She was ordered to put one of her children onto a waiting truck, but she could not do it. A Ukrainian stepped up to them and smashed the three of them over the head with an axe and threw their bodies onto the truck. That's what I remember about Tisha B'av. It's as clear to me as my hand. And what about the six million Jews? Why isn't there a day of fasting for them? For the destruction of the Temple, for the loss of stone and wood, we have to fast, but for six million Jews we do nothing! That's swept under the carpet. A little accident on the part of God. Well, no matter, we must go on!" Beryl spluttered bitterly, his small eyes narrowed, the corners of his mouth frothing.

"You're right," answered Zushe, to the stunned surprise of the onlookers, including Joseph. "You're absolutely right. There should be a memorial day for them."

"I don't mean a day for speeches!" exclaimed Beryl, still not placated.

"Neither do I."

"I mean a religious day, a day of fasting with special prayers and services."

"That's precisely what I mean," Zushe agreed, and with those words took the wind out of Beryl's sails.

It rained on Tisha B'av day. While the guests remained inside, Zushe paced the grounds, fasting, drenched. In the afternoon, he took his prayer shawl and tefillin and made his way to the forest behind the railroad tracks.

"Master of the Universe, help me, help me!" Zushe burst into tearful cries, hiding his head in his hands. "What do I do? Do I kill him to ease my pain? And will it ease the pain?"

Joseph had been hunting chipmunks in the forest nearby when he heard whimpering sounds. Shouldering his rifle, he cautiously followed the sounds into the bush. At the edge of a clearing, he saw Zushe sitting stooped on a tree stump, covered in a prayer shawl, phylacteries on his forehead and left arm.

Joseph made a rustling sound behind the trees. Zushe raised his head from beneath the prayer shawl. As he stood up, dressed in the full armour of his forefathers, his face shimmered in the fractured forest light. "Come here, Joseph," he called, extending both hands to him.

The boy stepped into the open, the rifle pointed down at his side.

"Can I help you?" Joseph asked, frightened by Zushe's wincing expression, but delighted by the opportunity to finally learn more about this mysterious man.

"No, no," Zushe whispered, quickly regaining his composure.

But Joseph saw through the feigned smile.

"You were talking about Beryl, weren't you? Something that happened during the war."

Zushe did not answer. He stepped towards the boy, gazing into his alert eyes. When he was within arms' reach, Zushe murmured in a self-deprecating tone, "The things that are truly important to me, those things I can't part with, those things I can't give Him. I wish I could. To God I give only my rags." As if to explain, he said, whispering, "A Jew isn't allowed to hate another—he must force himself to love him, no matter what. Love of a fellow human being means to love a hardened sinner the way you love a saint."

"It's Beryl, isn't it?" Zushe's silence then prompted the boy to say, "If not Beryl, it's my father. What did he do to you? Maybe there's good reason to hate him?"

Zushe didn't reply to the question. He removed his prayer shawl and phylacteries, then asked,

"Would you like to put the tefillin on now?"

"If you'd like me to," the boy replied, disappointed that Zushe would not confide in him.

Joseph put down his rifle on the grass, then took the tefillin bag from Zushe. He said the appropriate benediction then knowingly wrapped the black strap around his left arm. Zushe looked on with unconcealed pride as Joseph recited the Shma-Yisrael.

Sunday, late afternoon, Shloymeh stood on the patio shouting, "Minion! Minion!"

It was the anniversary of his mother's death and he needed a quorum of ten men to recite the Kaddish, the prayer for the dead. Although he had not said Kaddish for many years, Zushe had convinced him of its importance.

Ten men gathered in the dining room for the afternoon service. Now that Joseph was thirteen, he was counted among them. Zushe distributed skullcaps, then helped Shloymeh conduct the service.

"Thank you, thank you," Shloymeh said gratefully to each congregant individually when the service was completed.

The men dispersed quickly, happy to be done with the burdensome distraction. The skullcaps they had dutifully worn were dropped on the tables and the men hastened away.

Joseph went down to the dock. A tempestuous

grey sky puffed angrily over the lake. He wondered if he should try to swim across the lake. He had never done it before in a storm. But he wasn't wearing his bathing suit and he didn't feel like walking back to his room for it. When it started to rain, he returned to the hotel. As he was mounting the stairs to the patio, Mr. Dimant called to him from under the half-open awning, "Hey! Over there!"

Joseph saw him pointing to a bright green blob on the muddy walk below. At first glance he couldn't discern what it was. But suddenly he recognized the bright green skullcap Zushe had put on his head for the afternoon service and which he had forgotten to take off. Blushing, he went down the steps under the pelting rain and picked up the skullcap. Having inadvertently given Mr. Dimant the impression he had been wearing it, he felt there was no choice but to put it back on his head.

In the dining room, the guests grinned uneasily at the sight of Joseph with a skullcap. Crinkling up his nose, Professor Shpitzer observed: "What a pity, he could have grown up to be such a nice boy."

"Why are you doing this?" Mrs. Weinberg asked as she leaned towards him, genuinely puzzled. She sat tall in her chair, her hair braided into two high, symmetric challahs separated by a wide part in the middle. "I'm a Jew," he answered pluckily, but he could not conceal a troubled look.

"You don't have to wear a *kipa* to be a good Jew," Mr. Dimant declared. "Why, look at me!"

Rosenbloom entered the dining room. He had just returned from a walk with Beryl. He stepped around the tables, headed in the general direction of Joseph's table. Suddenly he noticed the skullcap on his head and gave a perceptible start. For a moment he tried to conceal his intense disquiet, then he grabbed the skullcap from his son's head and flung it away.

"Where is he?" he howled, clenching his fists, his lips trembling with rage. He stomped across the room to Zushe, who was sitting alone near the back windows, waiting for the guests to finish supper so he could start cleaning up. Zushe stood up to greet him. Rosenbloom did not slow down as he approached. His closed right fist smashed into Zushe's face without warning. Zushe's head swung around, but he stood his ground, blood gushing from his nose and mouth. Zushe nodded slowly and sat down. Freda ran to Zushe with a damp dish towel and pressed it to his nose.

"Why? Why, Asher? Why did you do this?" she wept.

Joseph came to the table and stood tremblingly between Zushe and his father.

Brandishing his arm, Rosenbloom warned in a staccato voice, "If you ever go near my son again, I'll kill you!"

"What does he want from us?" cried Beryl in a wail, waving his finger incriminatingly at Zushe. "We're good people! We're kind people!"

Zushe picked up the orange he had peeled seconds before Rosenbloom's attack, recited a blessing, and took a bite as though nothing had happened. Rosenbloom's glinting metallic eyes were still baring down on him. He was panting and grating his teeth. As Nora arrived with a bowl of warm water, Rosenbloom strode to the table where Joseph had been sitting, grabbed the rifle that was leaning against it, then ran back to Zushe. He pointed the barrel directly into Zushe's face and cranked the lever.

"Get up!" he commanded with burning eyes. "Get out of here! Move, you murderer!"

Zushe stood up, holding the towel to his face. For a moment, he gazed at Rosenbloom. It seemed as if he was about to say something, but he chose silence. A curious smile appeared on his lips, an incredible, knowing smile which puzzled the guests. Zushe's eyes met Joseph's in a glance of shared perception, then Zushe turned aside and walked towards the exit.

Now Rosenbloom turned on his son. With a mocking face, he ranted venomously.

"He stood at his mother's deathbed laughing, clapping his hands with joy! And now he wants to be a writer! An artist! To pull down his pants and dance naked on stage!"

The boy stared uncomprehendingly at his father, then ran out of the room.

In the middle of the night, when Asher's snoring had reached full stride, Joseph got dressed and tiptoed out of their room. He went to the third floor and knocked quietly on Zushe's door.

"Come in," Zushe called.

Joseph turned the knob and stepped into the dimly lit room. He was struck by the low slanting ceiling. The room was tiny and bare. Zushe was sitting on a small wooden box under a naked light, reading a holy book. His face was disfigured with swelling, and congealed blood lay clotted in his beard. There was no bed, only a thin mattress on the floor covered with a frayed woollen grey blanket.

"I'm sorry about my father," Joseph said.

"There's nothing to apologize for," Zushe said quietly.

"But your face."

"My face will heal," he reassured the boy, making little of the livid bruise on his cheek. "A Jew must know that it costs to do something for another Jew. He should be willing and happy to pay the price." There was compassion and mystery in his eyes. "Tomorrow the bruise will heal and no one will know anything happened." Joseph was perplexed by Zushe's words. "God tests us for our benefit, to strengthen us and to make us better people. Sure, He can give us that elevation without the test, but would we appreciate it then? And you, you must know that God is testing you through your father."

"I don't want the test and I don't want to forgive him! I hate him! He tortured my mother to death and now he's torturing me."

The boy was wearing the skullcap. Zushe pointed to it.

"You don't have to wear it for me."

"I do it for myself, not for you."

"All right, all right," he said, placing his hand lightly on the boy's shoulder.

Joseph looked around at the dirty walls of the room.

"Freda should have given you a better room," he said. "There's no bed, no table, nothing."

Zushe's lips widened into a painful, lopsided smile.

"This is not my home," he said. "Of course, in my home I'll have a chair, a bed, and a table. But here, in this world, a man is always on the move and all these physical things aren't important."

For the first time Joseph felt that Zushe had confided something very personal. The answer made him tremble because he knew that Zushe was talking about life and death. Zushe tried to assuage the severity of his words.

"A man travelling on a train does not need furniture, not even a change of clothing! A hard wooden seat will do."

"I understand."

"Come here," Zushe called to him.

Joseph stepped forward without fear. Zushe drew the boy close to him.

"God threw a handful of spice into a barrel of dust," he intoned in a melodious voice. "'Extract the spice from the dirt,' He commanded the Jews. 'Choose the good from the bad.' It sounds like an impossible task, but we can do it! God made it possible, because He gave us a very special instrument to do it with. He gave us the Torah."

"I know you could have hit my father back." Joseph reverted to the dining-room scene that still weighed heavily on him.

"If your foot slipped and you hurt yourself, would you punish your foot?" Zushe related words Mendl had once spoken to him in the iron mines. If only he meant them the way Mendl had. "When Beryl said the guests were good people, he was right. They are good people, Joseph. God built into every human being a capacity for being good. That capacity they have. But who is being good, they or God?" Zushe paused for a moment, then went on. "There are animals in the oceans called dolphins. If a dolphin is hurt, the others will endanger themselves to save the wounded dolphin. This is very noble, but can the dolphins be credited for being good? Of course not. They're only carrying out what God has built into their nature. It's the same with the guests. They are good, but only with the goodness that God gave them. They can't take credit for it; every bit of good they do is a result of instinct, not their own efforts."

"What difference does it make why a person does good so long as he does it?" Joseph asked, perturbed by what he understood to be only a technical distinction.

"If we do only what our instincts tell us—even if they are good instincts—then we don't grow, we don't become better people. To improve ourselves, we must go beyond our instincts, beyond the goodness with which we were born. We must use our brains. Often we have to do things that we would not like to do instinctively. To do these things we need intellect; we have to work with ourselves until the mind controls the instincts. That's the essence of serving God. And it isn't how much we actually accomplish that pleases God, but rather how sincere we are in our efforts."

As he was speaking, Zushe was filtering his words through his own life circumstances, trying to reconcile what he knew to be true with the pain in his heart that blocked the consequences of those words from applying to him personally. But how could he separate the two? How could he—as one prepared to kill—utter those saintly words to the boy? The argument he had used before—that although he himself was trapped in a quagmire, he nevertheless had the obligation to show others the way to safer ground—did not seem to him as strong as it once may have been.

It was after two o'clock.

"You have to get some sleep," Zushe said. "It's late."

"I'm fine."

"If your father gets up, he'll be very worried."

"I'll go, but only because I don't want to disturb you any more."

"No, no, you can never disturb me."

"One more question. Did you know my father during the war?"

"I'm not sure," Zushe said evasively.

"Then how did you know I had chicken pox in Germany?"

"Most children had," Zushe answered vaguely. "I guessed that you did also."

"And how did you know I was in the Frankfort DP camp?" the boy prodded.

"I overheard Freda talking to your father about it."

"Sure, sure," Joseph nodded suspiciously, but he did not force the issue further.

CHAPTER SIXTEEN

ROSENBLOOM'S attack on Zushe brought a subdued mood to the hotel. Although the day was still full of activity, occasionally an eerie stillness haunted the hotel in the evening. Faces looked withered and pinched, and overhead, flocks of seagulls appeared out of the clouds and flew in chaotic circles low over the hills near the hotel. Guests rested listlessly on the patio and on the front lawn, reticent, gazing at nothing in particular. Only Levy's despondent violin and the idle chatter of the cardplayers dared challenge the fretting silence.

A blistering heat wave engulfed the Laurentians in the third week of August. The smell of skunk floated over the beach. Ignoring it as best they could, a few guests waded into the lake to cool off from the dazzling sun, determined to get the most out of their hard-earned vacations.

One afternoon, Sollie went wobbling down to the beach, like a penguin in his black-and-white satin swim trunks.

"Not too far! Not too far!" he cautioned a girl of five or six, who was in the water up to her neck.

Clustered together like a school of fish, six women were treading water near the dock, chatting frivolously as they aimed their faces at the sun. Louis was in a bantering mood. The headwaiter appeared on the dock with a tray of cookies and tea, got down on his knees, placed the tray gently on the water, then pushed it towards the women.

"Teatime! Tea is now being served!" he called through megaphoned hands with an affected British accent.

In the late afternoon the stifling hot wind changed directions and now blew from the north. The high poplars along the beach front swayed towards the hotel. Louis appeared on the patio and stood impatiently clanging the bell. It was almost six o'clock, but dozens of guests still refused to leave the beach. The headwaiter curled his hands around his mouth and yelled.

"Last call for supper! The kitchen will be closed in precisely fifteen minutes! Last call!"

Finally the guests began to migrate towards the hotel, following two sandy paths up from the beach. In the dining room Mrs. Steiner was at war with the twins, who refused to eat their soup, determined only to lick the fluid off the noodles. Exhausted, Mrs. Steiner gave up and let them do what they wanted. As the guests streamed in to take their seats, the twins gazed into each other's eyes to see who would laugh first. They loved to play this game, especially with Beryl, who always engaged them with fervent earnestness, locking them in frozen, stalemated hour-long glares. Today, soon after Lea challenged him to a match, he burst into feigned laughter.

"All right, go out and play now," Mrs. Steiner announced with defeat as she wiped Lea's mouth with her open hand. But they didn't want to go. They remained sitting at their mother's table, scribbling numbers on each other's forearms with ballpoint pens Beryl had given them.

Nearby Shloymeh refused to touch his dessert. The recent violence in the hotel had disturbed him.

"What's wrong with you?" Sollie asked, gawking ravenously at Shloymeh's bowl of ice cream.

"Here, you can have it," he said, pushing the bowl to him.

Suddenly Shloymeh stood up. Those at his table thought that he was excusing himself, but he merely stood there, head bowed, his lips stirring soundlessly.

"I want to say something," he announced at length, choking with emotion.

The guests stopped eating and turned their attention towards Shloymeh.

"I can't keep it in any longer. It was in January of '43. I was in the train with my son," he said, catching his breath in sobs. "We were on the way to Treblinka. We had nothing to eat for two days. The train stopped near a farm in an open field. There was a plank on the floor that was loose. It was possible to get out, but I didn't know if I should go myself in the hope that I could bring food back before the train left, or if I should take my son and face starvation and frost in the forest. The boy was too weak to go, so the decision was made for me. I kissed him on the forehead and left the train. I'll never forget that moment." Shloymeh's quiet sobs reverberated through the hushed room. "When I came back, the train was gone."

Beryl crooked his arm around Shloymeh's and tried to lead him away, but he refused to move. Suddenly he barked a loud sneeze that settled slowly on the table. There was a momentary silence, then there came a more powerful sneeze. Shloymeh grasped the left side of his chest.

"Heart attack," Beryl announced.

A waiter slipped himself under Shloymeh's arm, barely keeping him from collapsing. Someone pushed a chair under Shloymeh's knees as the heavy man was lowered slowly into it.

"Get the dentist!" a woman shouted.

Freda spread a cold compress across Shloymeh's forehead. In an attempt to alleviate the despondent mood, Beryl reminded everyone that matters could be worse and indeed they were: a new case of polio had been discovered in Montreal and a Jewish boy at that.

"Shut up, you hypochondriac!" Mrs. Weinberg yelled at him. At last, Dr. Sacks arrived on the scene.

"My heart," Shloymeh whispered to the dentist.

As strident shadows blotted the eastern wall, Dr. Sacks sent everyone away except Beryl who was to serve as his assistant. Shloymeh was stretched out on a table. Beryl undid his shirt while the dentist prepared the stethoscope.

"Breathe normally," he ordered the patient.

The guests huddled silently near the lobby door as Dr. Sacks listened intently to Shloymeh's chest. Finally he plucked the stethoscope out of his ears and slapped Shloymeh on his sweaty hair-matted chest.

"You have a touch of bronchitis," the dentist stated his unequivocal diagnosis. "Your heart is perfect. I should have a heart like yours."

"Bronchitis?" asked Shloymeh, already feeling better.

"It's nothing—drink hot milk and you'll be all right."

"Why not hot tea?" Freda asked.

"Can't you forget about money for a minute?" Beryl admonished her publicly.

"Anything hot will be fine," the dentist said.

As Shloymeh sat up, coins fell out of his pocket and rolled across the dining-room floor in all directions, but he made no attempt to retrieve them.

CHAPTER SEVENTEEN

EARLY Sunday morning, Zushe walked slowly through the forest to the inlet he had used as a ritual immersion. The moment of truth was fast approaching, yet the sense of exhilaration he had imagined was lacking. For fifteen years he had grovelled in the details of the past. For fifteen years he had waited for this day, yet now it was not as he had planned. Rosenbloom was not simply a traitor, a betrayer of women and children. He was a man with a son. As pathetic a father as he was, the boy did have a roof over his head and the semblance of a family life.

After emerging from the lake, Zushe recited the morning prayers in the forest. He stood in front of a tree, his eyes closed, pouring his heart out to the Creator, begging for the strength to withstand the uncertainties of the coming days.

It was almost ten o'clock by the time he returned to his room. There was a note on the floor from Asher Rosenbloom requesting Zushe to meet him at seven o'clock in the evening behind the hotel. Zushe placed the bag containing the prayer shawl and phylacteries on the bed and left the room to prepare the dining hall for lunch.

By mid-afternoon Zushe was back in his room. He lay down on the mattress, his hands behind his head, and gazed at the ceiling as he recited Psalms from memory. The voices of the cardplayers on the patio below merged with the sounds of children on the beach. Zushe closed his eyes and prepared himself for the encounter with Asher.

Sharp stunted shadows pointed up the slope as Zushe walked to the meeting place behind the hotel. The terrain flattened out, flanked on both sides by evergreens and high bushes. Asher was waiting for him at the designated bench.

With rifle in hand Joseph was walking along the beach when he spotted a large frog hopping through the grass. Taking potshots at it, he followed it behind the hotel into the bushes lining the path up the hill. In the distance he heard men talking. On approaching, he recognized the voices of his father and Zushe. Asher was standing near a bench in a clearing. Zushe, at first sitting on the bench, stood up as they talked.

"Now I understand what's happening," Asher said with anger inflecting his voice. "You're holding my Joseph hostage. You want to know what happened after you left the cellar, and if you get the information you want, you'll let my son go. You're a good businessman!" Asher's voice was devoid of even a hint of apology for the attack in the dining room. "I've had time to think and I do remember more, but before I say anything we must make one thing clear: I'll tell you everything I know, but in return you'll order my son to come home with me tomorrow."

Zushe saw Rosenbloom as the murderous traitor his memory had portrayed him all these years. Whatever he promised such a man was devoid of meaning or obligation.

"Do you accept?" Asher pressed him.

Zushe nodded his agreement.

Zushe reminded him accusingly, "You remained in the cellar after the men left to find food. When we didn't return to the cellar after the first day, you sneaked out and made a deal with the Gestapo to save your family."

Asher sighed, then spoke in a low, confessional voice.

"It was an awful time. Good men became evil and even the most righteous men could not hold on to their sanity. We now rationalize and justify every decision we took, but in the end we were all evil, we acted cruelly, selfishly—you, me, all of us. That's nonsense! You don't really want to know what happened to your wife and children. If you knew the truth, you'd have no one to blame but yourself and your God. You're ashamed of your past. You think I don't remember that tramp coming into the cellar, half naked, starving? The way she threw herself at your feet in front of your wife."

That spectacle in the cellar, which Zushe had delegated to the deep recesses of his mind, suddenly flung him through the protective wall he had constructed around himself all these years.

"Yes, that woman who came for you. Such obscene language she used. But you remember all that better than I. No one could forget her. We all heard how you begged your wife to forgive you. And there she stood in front of everyone, your unexpected visitor. How fortunate you were that your children were too young to understand. No one had the heart to kick the tramp out, least of all you. Your poor wife—how she wept all night—and you begging her for forgiveness."

The sounds of a baby crying were heard from the hotel below, awakening Zushe's memory to the warm days in August 1939 when similar sounds were heard in his home. He recalled the strolls around the grounds of his home, a newborn daughter in his arms. Now his children would have been in their twenties, starting lives of their own. Had they survived the war, how would he face them with his shame? Gasping, Zushe tried to conceal his pain.

It was growing dark. From the hotel in the valley emanated a turbid light and now and then it entered the space between the two men, illuminating the intense features on their faces. Zushe stood in silence, stooped forward, entrapped by his past. He could not reply to Rosenbloom. Sensing his sudden advantage, Asher went on with anger and ridicule in his voice.

"Now I understand why you're here. You believe I betrayed your family and you've come to take away my Joseph to avenge your dead. A religious Jew, is that what you are? You're not angry with me. You're angry with God, but you don't dare express that anger, so you're tormenting me with my Joseph. That's your revenge. There was a storm. The bandits came and robbed the farm. You're not angry at the one who made the storm, you're not angry at the bandits—you're angry only at the person who may have accidently left the barn door open!"

A taunting grin covered his closely shaven face as he spoke, tiny foam bubbles bursting in the corners of his mouth.

"Yes, now I know the truth, you're here to kill, not because of what you think I did, but really to conceal your own crimes. I'm the only one alive who knows what you did to your wife and family. I am a witness—maybe the only one still alive—to your sins with the tramp. So now you've become a rabbi—from an adulterer to a saint! Quite a transformation, Katznelson!"

Zushe was uncertain about what had seemed to him so logical for fifteen years. Crushed by the accusation, he wondered, who was more worthy of punishment—Asher at the hand of Zushe or Zushe at the hand of God?

Asher went on with imposing confidence. "I have kept my side of the deal. I have told you all that I know. You're a religious Jew. You must keep your word. My son will leave with me in the morning."

Suddenly Joseph stepped into the open. The boy stood gazing at Zushe, tears streaming from his eyes.

"I thought you were my friend!" the boy cried at Zushe, his face contorted in anguish. "You double-crossed me! I mean nothing to you! You treat me no better than he does! Someone to be used and then thrown away!"

The boy stopped shouting, threw a blazing look at Zushe, and ran into the woods.

In the ensuing days Joseph avoided Zushe. He ate his meals quickly and left the dining hall before there was the slightest opportunity for even eye contact with Zushe. He resumed the frog hunting he had stopped for a week. Scouring the lake for traces of frog life, he discovered new breeding grounds in swamps along shores he had not visited before. The slaughter continued and with it the boy's disappointment and anger towards both his father and Zushe.

One rainy afternoon Zushe stood on the deserted patio combing his beard with his knuckles. He was waiting for Joseph to come up from the beach where he had tied up the rowboat on his return from a hunt. The boy's disillusion troubled Zushe.

"Will you ever give me a chance to defend myself?" Zushe called to him. "Even a murderer is given a chance to speak in court."

"You used me all this time just to get information out of my father! Are you happy now?" he blurted out as he turned the corner, taking the long way around the hotel to avoid Zushe.

Joseph returned late that evening from the direction of the town. There was only one poker game in progress. Beryl was sitting slouched, legs crossed, yawning. No one took notice of the distraught expression on the boy's pallid face. Beryl nodded a greeting.

Joseph smiled blandly, then entered the lobby where Asher was sitting on a sofa reading a Yiddish newspaper. The boy didn't want to stay there, for fear of confronting his father to whom he had not spoken since the incident with Zushe. He heard Freda talking to Zushe in the dining hall. Still angry with Zushe, he returned to the patio. He stepped to the edge of the balustrade and gazed into the darkness. A moth hovered under the light bulb, casting magnified shadows haphazardly across the patio. A bonfire on the front lawn was still burning, tall ghost-birches huddled behind it. Joseph glanced at the clearing sky, illuminated in the north by a bright full moon. How utterly alone he felt. Zushe, on whom he had placed so much hope, was exactly as Beryl had claimed him to be at the beginning of the summer. There were no real saints in the world—everyone had his personal reasons for pretending to be nice. But no one really was. And yet what hurt him the most was not so much a feeling of being exploited as a sensation of being rejected. His mother had rejected him by her death, his father hated him, and now Zushe had thrown him away for his own selfish reasons. It hardly mattered what those reasons were.

The last poker game was over. The players collected their money from the table and stepped wearily towards the lobby door. Only Beryl remained sitting, frowning in misery against the burps rising inexorably from his stomach. Joseph did not want to talk. At length Beryl stood up.

"*Nu*, how is the writing progressing?" he called to the boy. "I do want to see the manuscript before the end of the summer. Please help me to my room—I feel so weak."

Joseph dashed to Beryl's side. He curled his arm around Beryl's shoulders and helped him to his feet.

The guests were enjoying the pleasant mid-August weather. Appetites were hearty, virtually obscene, and between meals the beach and front lawn were crowded with sun lovers. The summer was slipping away, but it could still be savoured by a swim or a leisurely walk around the lake. In the evenings, the awning was rolled up and the guests sat on the patio sipping lemonade under clear skies. The occasional leaf falling on the front lawn was a dismal reminder of things to come, but it also inspired the guests to delight in every breath of fresh air, every moment of calm and repose.

Only the twins refused to accede to the peaceful atmosphere at the hotel. In spite of Freda's repeated assurances, they remained convinced the food was not kosher. Like Zushe, they ate mostly fruits and vegetables and drank water with their hands, refusing to use the hotel's cups. Zushe insisted that certain foods were now kosher, but they didn't believe a word he said. In desperation, Mrs. Steiner filled the holes of dried cereal with mashed chicken and chased her starving daughters around the hotel grounds.

Joseph refused to talk to Zushe and even to Freda,

who went out of her way to serve him personally in the dining room. He walked about in a dismal silence, alienated from the adult guests whom he had once viewed as his friends.

Freda went to great lengths to keep the hotel clean and free of rodents, but despite her best efforts a mouse found its way into the kitchen during the Sabbath lunchtime meal. From there it scurried into the dining room, throwing the guests into panic. In a state of utter bedlam, the guests left the compote and cake and swarmed through the lobby onto the patio and front lawn. Men, women, and children stood in disarray on the front lawn in a scene reminiscent of wartime. Freda ordered Louis to go inside and chase the mouse out. She handed him a broom and pointed him in the direction of the dining room.

"It's your job! You have to do it!"

Louis entered the lobby, resigned to his fate.

"Keep the door open," he called to one of the waiters.

A few minutes later, Louis's voice was heard: "Get out! Get out! Shoo! Shoo!"

A grey mouse appeared on the patio, where the bright sunlight made it stop abruptly. As it looked around, dazed, Joseph, who was down on one knee with shouldered rifle, pulled the trigger. The mouse fell over and lay twitching on the wooden floor.

Rosenbloom rushed out of the crowd on the front lawn, leaped up the steps, and grabbed the mouse by the tail. Displaying it to the crowd, he exclaimed wildly: "This is how he killed his mother!"

The accusation stunned the boy. Although he had heard it often enough before in different contexts, it infuriated him. The allegation had never accorded with his memories but, caught red-handed as he had been now, killing an animal, he could hardly refute the charge of murder. Joseph jumped down from the patio and ran through the crowd to the back of the hotel. Zushe, who had been walking behind the hotel, saw the fury on the boy's face and tried to reach out to stop him, but Joseph brushed past him as he darted towards the road.

"He's going to kill himself! I know him, he'll do it!" Rosenbloom sobbed pathetically as he chased his son. "What have I done? What have I done?"

Zushe ran after Rosenbloom, soon overtaking him. One after the other, they thrashed through a shoulder-high cornfield that had been recently harvested. Every few moments, Zushe slowed down to locate the boy over the swaying, bristling husks. Joseph was heading towards the cliffs near the town.

When Zushe reached the pool beneath the cliffs, he could not locate Joseph. Huge boulders jutted out from the steep mountain face like clenched fists, threatening to fall into the cesspool below. Zushe searched the surroundings, but there was no sign of the boy. On the road below him, he heard Rosenbloom advancing, cursing Zushe and his son.

Suddenly Joseph appeared on the top of the ridge. He stood on a boulder, inching his way towards the edge.

"Get back!" Zushe yelled. "Get back! I order you!"

The boy did not answer. Zushe assessed the chances of scaling the mountain directly—the circuitous route around the back of the mountain would take too long. Without equipment it seemed impossible. There was a line of shrubbery among the boulders extending almost to the top. If he followed the bushes, there was a chance of scaling the cliff. Zushe threw off his hat and jacket and started up the slope, his skullcap falling off with the first leap.

"Wait for me!" Rosenbloom screamed, running after Zushe. "I killed my own son! I killed him!"

Zushe climbed the first forty feet without difficulty. From a narrow ledge, Joseph came more fully into view. He now stood on the very edge of the cliff, leaning towards the pool.

"Wait!" Zushe shouted at him.

"For your mother's sake!" Rosenbloom cried, standing about fifty feet below Zushe. "Have mercy on your mother, Joseph! Have mercy!"

Suddenly, the shrub Asher was clasping gave way.

He staggered and fell backwards over the side. Turning in midair, he fell screaming into the pool. One arm emerged from the water, then he went under and came up on his back.

Zushe stood frozen on a tiny ledge of earth, clinging to a branch. Jewish law exempted him from any effort on a traitor's behalf, but Zushe could not exempt himself. He ran down the mountain face, slipping and falling as he careered down the treacherous slope. Within seconds, he had reached the pool. Rosenbloom was about thirty feet away. Zushe kicked off his shoes as he plodded into the muddy pool. Leaning into the odorous water, he thrashed towards the floating body. Water filled his nostrils, cutting into his throat with the sharpness of a blade.

Rosenbloom was unconscious when he reached him. Zushe curled his arm around the man's neck and tried to keep his head out of the water. But the heavy body craved for the depths of the pool. He glimpsed Asher's livid, disfigured face, his wide-open eyes staring at the sun, and he couldn't tell whether he was alive or dead. He knew only that he had to bring him out. With a surge of renewed strength, Zushe tightened his grip, slipping him onto his back, his left arm around Asher's neck. As Zushe's legs thrashed away, they began moving towards the shore, barely afloat.

Joseph was standing among the trees a good way off when Zushe staggered out of the pool on his knees.

"Run to the hotel! Get help!" Zushe commanded, but the boy wouldn't move.

Zushe turned Asher on his stomach and began striking his back with open hands. When Asher failed to regain consciousness, Zushe turned him onto his back and pressed hard into his chest with the palms of his hands. Suddenly Asher opened his eyes.

"Forgive me, forgive me," Asher whispered, unaware that Joseph stood behind him. "I too had a family. I tried to save my children. Forgive me. I never meant to harm the others. I only wanted to save my children." Asher's eyes curled beneath the lids as he lost consciousness.

"Save him, God! Save him!" Zushe pleaded. He fell on Asher's shrivelled blue lips, breathing hard into him. Rosenbloom did not stir, but Zushe refused to give up.

"Go now!" he yelled at Joseph, who stood dazed at the edge of the pool. With streaming eyes, the boy stepped up to his father, bent down, and stroked his head again and again. Looking up plaintively at Zushe, the boy saw his exposed forearm and the numbers inscribed along the inside.

Zushe enunciated to the boy with ineffable urgency: "Run, it's for your father!"

Joseph now responded, leaping like a fawn over fallen trees, quickly disappearing in the bush.

Zushe breathed with all his strength into Asher's mouth.

"Please, God, save him!" A desperate supplication was torn from him. "For my sake! Do it for my sake!"

A gurgle was heard. Zushe did not know from whom it came. A wheezing sound reverberated between the two men, then a cough came up from the body, another and still another, stronger and stronger, and Zushe felt something heavy and painful rise from him. He closed his eyes and breathed shallowly, and when he again opened his eyes, he was no longer hateful towards Asher nor was he angry with God. A part of him had died, but a pain was lifting from him, rising amorphously with the hushed Psalms seeping through his trembling lips.

Zushe thought in his heart, Acceptance of the past, this would be my gift to God. But he knew that for him it was more than rags, more, much more.

Asher's eyelids parted and he saw Zushe sitting beside him in mud. Zushe leaned Asher's head against his thigh and for the first time in as long as he could remember he felt calm within himself.

CHAPTER EIGHTEEN

ASHER did not return to the city Monday morning even though there were many lifts available with the departing guests this last week of August. That evening, a few cardplayers gathered in the dining room where Zushe was clearing away the supper dishes. Someone had brought a bottle of whisky and the men drank as they played poker.

"Come, let's make a toast," Shloymeh called to Zushe, brandishing a forty-ounce bottle.

To everyone's surprise, Zushe accepted the invitation. He took a half-full glass from Shloymeh's hand, recited the appropriate benediction, and drank it down. Two players pushed their chairs aside to make room for him at the table.

It was remarkable that whisky never upset Beryl's stomach. Having had a few drinks, Beryl was in a cheerful mood. With a grin on his pallid face, he mused aloud: "We believed too much in miracles—that was our greatest mistake. If not for that, millions of Jews would have survived. Until the last moment we believed a miracle would save us. I remember in my shtetl when hundreds of Russian soldiers lay dead in the streets, and not a single Jew dared touch their weapons. Taking action would have interfered with the divine plan. It's incredible, but that's what we believed until the last breath! No one dared lift a finger in self-defence!"

"That's not true," Shloymeh disagreed.

"Later there was some resistance by a few," Beryl conceded with a wave of the hand. "But it's true, the masses went obediently to their deaths. We were in a stupor, a stupor created by thousands of years of Torah study."

Zushe sat in silence, gazing wistfully past the players at the windows facing the back lawn and the forest beyond. From time to time, someone handed him a glass of whisky.

"There were miracles," Shloymeh said, as if to support the objection in Zushe's silence. "The Germans attacked Poland on Sunday. Monday they were already in my shtetl. There was no time to think, never mind to act. The rabbi of our shtetl and I escaped to the forest. Moishe Kessler was his name. Where can one find a man like him today? 'Shloymeh,' he said to me, 'a black cloud is about to engulf our people. Run, run wherever your feet will carry you. Whenever you'll be in danger, recite this verse from Psalm Thirty-two and no harm will befall you: "You are shelter for me. From distress You preserve me. With glad song of rescue You envelope me."' I did as he told me. How many times I lay in trenches, bullets whizzing around me, people being killed left and right. I recited the verse over and over again, and you see I came out of the war without a scratch. The verse saved me, but it didn't work for the rabbi. The Ukrainians broke into the synagogue and stabbed him in the back as he stood at his lectern praying. Is that justice for you, I ask?"

"Of course there were miracles," Beryl acknowledged, "but they were few and far between. I'll tell you one that happened to me. There were three of us hiding in the forest: Pesach Mulchewski, Nachum Rosenblatt, and myself. It was December and bitterly cold. We had worked late into the night building a shelter. About midnight we went to search for food. It was impossible to go out in the day. There was a farm a few miles away. Nachum said he knew the owner. We decided to take our chances. On the way there, we had to cross a river. The day before, we had seen children playing on the ice, so we thought it was safe. Halfway across, Pesach fell in. He came up once and that was the last we saw of him. Nachum and I couldn't do anything for him. We stepped carefully around the hole in the ice and continued towards the shore. Nachum made it to safety, but about ten yards from the shore the ice broke beneath my feet and I fell in. I held on to the ice to keep from sinking, but every time I tried to raise my leg the ice I was holding broke off from the main sheet. As the hole grew bigger, the current began pushing me downstream. I could no longer feel my legs. There was nothing Nachum could do. We decided he should try to get help from the farmer. Two hours later they came back—Nachum together with a father and his two sons. They had brought long poles with them which they extended to me under my arms. But my clothes were frozen solid and the poles kept slipping through. I couldn't hold out much longer. The Gentile had an idea: Nachum should lie down on the two poles and crawl out to me over the ice; he would take hold of me and the Gentiles would pull both of us in. Believe it or not, it worked. It was an open miracle. The Gentiles took me to their farm and brought me back to life. You see, there were good Gentiles. How many Jews would have risked their lives for a Gentile?"

Shloymeh filled the glasses again.

"To life!" he toasted in his maudlin voice, scratching his big stuck-out ears with his free hand.

"To life! To life!" the men responded.

Sollie, who had entered the room only minutes

earlier, gathered his stomach around him on the chair, and began to reminisce.

"I was running in the forest all day. Then I wasn't as fat as I am today. Towards evening I fell down and couldn't get up. I knew that my life was in great danger but I couldn't move. I fell asleep in the open. Then my dead father came to me in a dream. There was a German standing nearby with his rifle pointed at me. As he was about to pull the trigger, my father stepped between us and threw a flame of fire into his face. The German stepped aside, again aiming his rifle at me. But my father wouldn't let him kill me. Time and time again, he stepped between us and threw flames of fire at the German. When I awoke it was night. Later I learned that German patrols had passed within feet of where I was lying. My father's soul had protected me."

With tears in his eyes, Shloymeh proposed another toast. "Only we know what it means to have lived through the war. No one else can possibly understand. Let's drink to the Jewish heroes!"

Zushe did not relate any of the miracles that had brought him through the war. He did not say a word, but his newfound peace among these men, which everyone felt, spoke for him.

After supper Tuesday evening Joseph accompanied his father to a waiting car. Asher looked pale and weak. He walked with a stoop, carrying a valise and shopping bags in his left hand. He was returning to the city, but Joseph would stay on a few more days.

"Don't forget to do the rolls," Rosenbloom reminded him, referring to the socks filled with change he had left for Joseph to roll up.

"I'll do it, don't worry," Joseph assured him.

Near the car, Asher bent down to kiss the boy, his mouth wide open, clumsy as always, tears streaming down his unshaven cheeks. Today, Joseph did not resist.

Zushe appeared.

"Have a safe trip," he said cordially, his hand outstretched.

Asher nodded and took the hand in his.

"You'll keep an eye on the boy until I return?"

"Yes, of course," Zushe replied, putting his arm around Joseph's shoulder.

In the evening, Zushe saw Joseph walking towards the road. He caught up to him near the inlet and greeted him with a friendly hello, but Joseph responded with an icy nod.

"You're still angry with me," Zushe remarked.

"Not angry, just disappointed."

"Because I'm human like everyone else?"

"You were ready to destroy our friendship to get what you wanted from my father. Is that why you were friendly with me all summer, so you could use me? It was all a trick, wasn't it? Beryl was right all along."

"I didn't trick you. Certain things happened. I'd like to explain."

"You don't have to. I don't have to know everything. I don't really want to know."

Zushe gazed at the boy with affection. Their eyes met and Joseph saw pain and a regret that could not be bound in words.

They walked to the bend in the road and stopped. Zushe turned to the lake. The water splashed gently against the rocky shore thirty feet below. Beyond the distant hills, the sun was setting amid creeping, misty clouds. Zushe wanted to speak to him as he did earlier in the summer, and although he feared it might cause more damage than good, he would try.

"Once at a gathering of Chassidic Jews in Russia, someone was sent down to the cellar to bring up wine. When he entered the cellar, the young man cried out, 'It's pitch black down here!' From upstairs, there was a shout, 'That's only in the beginning. Later, when you get used to it, it becomes bright.' Do you understand, Joseph? We're living in darkness, a double darkness, and I—I admit it openly—am part of that darkness. It's bitterly dark in the world—there's so little Torah in it—but we're so used to it that we call it light." Zushe turned his expressive eyes on the boy, but it was not as before between them.

"I'm going back to high school," Joseph said, holding his shoulders back.

"I know."

"I want a profession. Maybe after I'll go to a yeshiva. I don't know—we'll see."

"You don't have to explain, Joseph."

"I want to."

"There's no need to. Our friendship doesn't depend on what you do. We're friends no matter what."

No matter what. The words rang in Joseph's ears. It would be good to know that there was someone out there who cared for you no matter what. But he wondered if Zushe really meant it. The boy glimpsed Zushe's eyes, squinting against the last rays of sunlight. Maybe it was not entirely as he saw it, Joseph thought. Zushe had once said, "Maturity means to go on, not to dwell on interpretations." Perhaps that's what he had to do now?

A crescent moon swayed among the crowns of the high poplars.

"Soon it will be Rosh Hashanah—a New Year, Joseph."

The boy nodded. Zushe put his arm around his shoulders and led him towards the hotel.

Friday evening, after the Sabbath candles had been lit, Zushe went to a table near the back of the deserted dining hall where he had prepared wine and challah. The guests had eaten long before. He recited the benediction for the wine, then washed his hands in the kitchen. When he returned, he found Freda sitting at his table, wearing a dress he had never seen before. Her hair was concealed beneath a violet kerchief and her face looked younger, even radiant. He cut the challah and bit slowly into the slice.

"Good *Shabbes*," she said when he looked up at her. "Am I disturbing you?"

"No, not all."

"Can I bring you something? A tea?"

"No, thank you."

After he finished chewing the mouthful of challah, he immediately recited grace.

"This wasn't a meal," she declared in reprimand. "I eat because I'm hungry. You eat for other reasons."

"Would you like to go for a walk?" he asked, standing up. "There's still some daylight left."

"I'd love to."

They followed the path through the back lawn to the road, then walked uphill away from the lake. The road narrowed into a path which traversed meadows, ending abruptly high in the hills overlooking a valley. Green and yellow fields shimmered in the oblique sunlight, and along the northern horizon the mountain coping bristled with evergreens, like the manes of frightened cats. Towards the lake, a beautiful panorama greeted them: silos and barns lay strewn across the shadowed evening landscape, slender roads meandering through the hills.

Far below them the partially visible hotel appeared tiny. Zushe thought about the men and women inside, and the pain of memory that seethed within those wooden walls. A chill went through him as he chased his galloping thoughts. There was something fantastic going on before his eyes, something that transcended the survivors and their suffering.

"What are you thinking, Zushelle?" Freda whispered, standing at his side.

"I should have done more for the guests," he said with regret. "If they leave the hotel as naked as they came, it'll be entirely my fault." He was thinking in particular about his failure with Joseph. If he hadn't given in to his self-gratification, the boy would not have seen him in his terrible weakness.

"You did your best," Freda said.

"I didn't do my best and that's why nothing was accomplished," Zushe said with certainty.

"How can you say that? The hotel food is now kosher; there's a mezuzah on the front door. Is that nothing? Zushe, don't forget what these people have lived through. You did do your best—that's all that matters. Don't worry about Joseph. He'll turn out just fine. His mother's soul is watching over him. I feel it."

As they walked on in the twilight, she took his hand. It felt limp and soft in hers, neither giving itself to her nor resisting.

"I've been thinking you should take up your profession again," she suggested courteously. "You were a teacher for many years, why give it up?"

Zushe looked at her with surprise.

His profession! How strange those words sounded to him—as though he was a man with a normal life to whom such a phrase might have meant something, as though he was no longer the vagabond into which the war had shaped him. For years he hadn't thought about his once-beloved profession of teaching. To indulge in such thoughts now required a commitment to live. Inured as he had grown to fumbling through the mangled semblance of life that resided in his memory, could he indeed survive outside the past? Perhaps it was only there, among the frozen images of his wife and children, that he could ever find solace?

Off to their right, a road lamp diluted the thickening dusk.

"I have a few dollars saved up," Freda said. "You could go back to university and take refresher courses, to learn French maybe. You know French is very important in this province. I'm not a smart woman, but I know it's important for you to have a higher education."

She drew closer to him in the darkness. When he glimpsed her face in the moonlight, he saw the wincing expression around her eyes.

"I know I'm not pretty—my skin is so bad and I'm not smart—no match for your intelligent mind. But I could help you quietly in your work, behind the scenes so to speak. It would be a business partnership. Oh, I know I could never replace your wife—I wouldn't want to try. Only it doesn't make sense—I mean, to live separately. In the summers, you'd help me in the hotel."

He nodded thoughtfully, his lips quivering, reciting Psalms out of fear, a grin of painful self-knowledge suffusing his face.

"I know you're afraid. But I'm the one who should be afraid, not you. A woman gives herself completely to a man—she won't leave him if something goes wrong. A man is capable of leaving a woman and that's why he feels the woman thinks the same as him. I don't know if I'm saying it clearly, Zushe. I was never good at speaking. I always spoke from the heart, not from the head. What I'm trying to say is that you shouldn't worry that I'm not getting a whole person—I don't want such a person. I want you as you are."

He saw her hair sticking out from beneath the

kerchief; it was white around the temples. Now she looked her years. He wanted to be able to gaze past her physical presence and see the kind, suffering person she was. Then he could love her for her essence, unhindered by appearances, by what she did or said. Then he could look at her the way God must have looked at him when He brought him through the tempest.

Freda was a woman keenly sensing her belated chance at happiness. The unaffected simplicity of her character pierced the citadel of his self-knowledge. There was something to her simple arguments, he thought. A man with time to explore the details of life did not live properly. Perhaps he had thought too much about life, about marriage?

Near the hotel, cheerful voices were heard from the front lawn. He cast a benevolent glance at her and she answered it with much, much more. The couple stopped on the road overlooking the inlet. The water glistened, dancing little crests skimming towards the beach.

"How beautiful the Sabbath is," Freda murmured with a rapturous sigh.

Sunday afternoon Zushe went for a walk around the lake with Joseph and Gerald. They walked slowly so as not to strain the crippled youth. Zushe told them a story he had heard from an old man in Jerusalem.

"Escaping Nazi-occupied Poland, a group of young Chassidic boys on their way to Russia stopped for a night in a shtetl," Zushe began in a quiet but intense voice. "They had heard that it was possible to reach America through Shanghai. The rabbi of the town was very hospitable to them. The boys told him of their plan to go to America. The rabbi thought long about it, then told them a story about dogs. These were special dogs trained to perform in a circus. One was dressed as a general, another as a major, and still another as a captain. During performances they paraded about in full military attire, in regimental order, saluting each other with raised paws. It cost ten rubles to get into the circus and many people couldn't afford such a large sum. A certain man was very upset that he couldn't get in. He climbed up a tree overlooking the circus grounds and waited for the performance to begin. When the military parade began, he threw a bag of meat in front of the dogs. They immediately broke rank and jumped for the food. Needless to say, the performance was completely disrupted, replaced by a vicious fight for the meat."

Zushe paused. They continued a few steps down the dusky road, the high birch trees on the slopes to their left lit up by the flat evening sunlight. Zushe resumed the story.

"The rabbi of the shtetl looked at the boys and

said: 'You must always remember that you are trained to be soldiers in God's army. In America you will experience many new things. Be on guard that the meat, the wealth of America, should not destroy you.'"

Although the sight of his father aiming the barrel at Zushe's face had aroused in Joseph an aversion towards the rifle, he was not quite ready to part with it. One afternoon he met Gerald on the dock, where he had been practising the accordion.

"Look!" he shouted to Joseph, pointing to a humming bird perched prominently on a summer chair between the dock and patio. Joseph acknowledged the information and was about to move on when Gerald dared him: "Aren't you going to shoot it?"

"I don't kill innocent birds!" Joseph snapped back.

"You murdered a million frogs in the lake and now you're chicken to kill a single bird! What a hypocrite, man!"

The accusation infuriated Joseph. He lay down on the grass, shouldered the rifle, and took aim. The line of sight extended beyond the bird to the third-floor windows of the hotel.

"Shoot!" Gerald goaded him.

Joseph squeezed the trigger slowly and sent the bird toppling over onto the grass.

For a moment, the bird lay still in the grass, then it leapt up in an attempt to fly, but it could only hop pathetically around, squealing softly.

"Right through the wing!" Gerald screamed, then hobbled to the bird.

As Joseph lay on the grass, something impinged upon the upper extremity of his vision: Zushe was standing behind the window of his room, looking down on the front lawn, his prayer shawl cowled over his head. Joseph gave a start. Blushing, he stood up. With the rifle pointed downward, his body shielding it from Zushe's view, he walked quickly towards the back lawn.

CHAPTER NINETEEN

Mrs. Steiner and the twins were packed and ready to return to the city, but the weather in the last days of August was so wonderful she decided to stay until the very last day of the season. The prospect of leaving made Lea irritable and the slightest incident set her off. She accused Rochl of looking at her, but Rochl denied it to her face. Whenever her mother mentioned their departure, Lea threatened, "If we go, I'm never going to change my panties!"

The dentist had already spent much more time at the hotel than he had planned. With his golf bag strapped across his shoulder, he went to the lobby to bid farewell to his good friends.

"Now we'll be all alone," an elderly woman

sobbed convulsively. "Who will take care of us?"

"I left my phone number with Freda," he consoled her, his hand on her shoulder. "You can call me anytime, night or day."

"You mean your office is in your house?" someone asked.

"Yes, didn't you know? On Esplanade, at the corner of Duluth."

All at once the guests wanted to know more about him. Was he married? Did he have children? If so, why didn't he bring them to the country with him? Why didn't he ever speak about them?

But there was no time for answers now. The dentist's green Studebaker was warming up, the trunk open, ready to receive the golf clubs. Accompanied by Louis, who was carrying the valises, and Beryl, Dr. Sacks approached his car. There he turned around and waved to his adoring fans on the patio. Beryl extended his right hand to the dentist.

"You must understand that the colon is not an iron pipe," the dentist said. "You have spasms there; that's the source of all your abdominal pain. You've got to relax your colon." Dr. Sacks held his closed fists side by side, and turned them in opposite directions as he had done so often in recent weeks to explain the nature of the spasms in the large intestine. "Relax it, once and for all! You can do it! It depends only on you! I honestly believe that your colon is more nervous than you. Your colon is in your head. But, anyhow, you are feeling better, Beryl," Dr. Sacks stated happily. "Admit it, Beryl. Be a man and admit it." Beryl nodded halfheartedly. "You see, our efforts were not in vain. Don't forget the headstands two hours after meals. That'll get the gas out of the colon and back into the duodenum. I know this isn't a complete cure, but it'll help you bear the symptoms until they go away. Relax, Beryl, and your colon will relax with you."

"Thank you, Doctor, thank you," Beryl muttered gratefully.

As they embraced, Beryl belched into the dentist's ear, but there was no harm done. Dr. Sacks beamed joyously one last time towards the patio, then got into the car. As he was about to start the motor, he realized that he had forgotten something.

"Louis!" he called to the headwaiter, who had been standing expectantly nearby like a puppy. He reached into his pocket and took out a twenty-dollar bill. Louis took it appreciatively, then stepped away from the car.

On his last trip to Montreal, Dr. Sacks had bought a used television set as a present for the hotel. Although it worked fine in the store, when it was installed in the lobby only snow appeared on the screen. With Nora back in Montreal, there was no entertainment and many of the remaining guests went to hear Zushe's Torah lessons.

In the dining hall, the round tables were arranged around Zushe like the petals of a flower, the guests sitting on the outside of the large circle. Before Zushe could get started this evening, Professor Shpitzer stood up. He glanced at the guests and began to speak in a ridiculing voice.

"Now I would like to ask you what you think of Darwin's theory of evolution. Surely you believe in it! Which intelligent man doesn't?"

"No, I don't believe in Darwin or his theory," Zushe said with a trace of resentment. "But I won't debate that issue with you now. Let me only say a word about what that theory has done for mankind. When a man believed that he originated from God, he had someone to look up to, to emulate. He looked up at God and knew that he had to strive to be a kind person. But now that he believes his great-grandfather was a gorilla, he emulates the gorilla—he becomes the gorilla. Why not—his great-grandfather was one?"

Professor Shpitzer grinned, at a loss for words. Noticing the indifferent response of the guests to his line of questioning, he sat down. Joseph entered the room and sat down behind Zushe.

"Rabbi," said Sollie, swallowing the last morsel of his apple strudel. "There's one thing I'd like to ask, which is actually quite important. A few days ago you talked about the four groups of Jews—remember?"

"Yes."

Zushe did not mind the interruptions. He was happy that guests were attending his Torah classes. That was an accomplishment at the Four Leaf Clover Hotel.

"When they came out of Egypt and saw this big ocean, none had the right answer as to what to do," Sollie went on, fired by a sudden enthusiasm for the subject matter he vaguely remembered from his school days. "One group said we should fight, one said we should pray, and God told them to shut up. Am I right, Rabbi?"

"More or less." Zushe smiled.

"The third group said we should go back to Egypt, and the fourth group said we should throw ourselves into the sea. Is that correct?" Sollie asked.

"Yes, Sollie."

"And none had the right answer?"

"That's right."

"What I'd like to know is, where did the answer come from?"

"That's a good question, Sollie," Zushe said. "First, let's try to understand why the four suggestions were wrong. To fight is not the goal of a Jew; while fighting Egyptians we can be killed ourselves. We have more important things to do. The second group prayed and God told them to be quiet, because prayer without action is meaningless. The third group wanted to drown themselves. Did God lead them out of Egypt to have them drown in the sea? This showed complete lack of faith in God. And the last group said, 'Let's go back to Egypt.' This was the most faithless proposal of all. God had just freed them from Egypt, and now they wanted to become slaves again. The fundamental error in all the suggestions was that although they may have been logical, they lacked faith in God."

"And that wasn't good, Rabbi?"

"That's right, it wasn't good."

"So logic was zero then? It's logical that you can't cross a sea. So what happened? Did Moses have the answer?" Sollie asked, feeling that at last he was on the verge of being understood.

"Moses didn't have the answer either. The Jews should have tried to cross the sea with the belief that God would help them. God had just freed them; He had performed miracle after miracle for them and still they didn't trust Him."

It was remarkable that Zushe was able to talk to the survivors about the Torah and God as though nothing had happened in the last twenty years. His words denied the survivors the refuge of self-pity for the atrocities they had lived through. By simply ignoring the terrible years, he had short-circuited that awful part of their collective memory. He related only to the recollections of their youths in prewar Poland, years saturated with Torah and the shtetl life that had been so securely supported by it.

Zushe gazed thoughtfully at their weary, questioning faces.

"We must always remember that the Torah is not simply a story," he said. "Every line, every word carries a direct message for each and every one of us all the time. The meaning in the crossing of the sea is that there is a sea, a spiritual sea, in every Jew."

"We all have it," Sollie concurred.

"When we're confronted by it, the only thing to do is to go forward. Once we've made that decision, God will split the sea for us as He did for Moses and the Jews at that time."

"In other words, you need guts!" Sollie blurted out, and in his excitement slapped Shloymeh hard on the back. His ruddy cheeks sweating, Sollie felt duty bound to explain: "Each Jew is an entity onto himself, right, Rabbi? He's capable, if he wants, of turning a whole country upside down. Because why? Because he's illogical. If you're logical, you know you can't turn a country upside down, but since we're illogical that's why we survived as a race."

"Some survival," observed Mrs. Weinberg, daintily touching up the corners of her lips.

Sollie looked around at the others for approval,

then clumsily lifted cake crumbs off the table with his dampened fingertips.

"A Jew also has to be logical," said Zushe. "He has to support a family, he has to care for himself, he has to be responsible. These all require logic."

"Of course!" trumpeted Sollie, as though Zushe had fully corroborated his own words.

Freda stood up to bring more cake and tea. Sollie offered to help, but she gestured for him to remain sitting.

"It takes years of practice to reach your soul," Mrs. Steiner affirmed with a heavy sigh.

"Definitely, definitely, without the badness the goodness is nothing," Mrs. Weinberg claimed with deep conviction. She looked around for endorsement, but the statement had fallen upon deaf ears.

Autumn had tossed its gauntlet across the front lawn, big red leaves strewn in serried heaps here and there. The days were growing shorter and the sun struggled against a frequently mirthless sky. Seagulls, pompous puffs of white, puttered about the front lawn, pecking into the charred wood at the bonfire sites.

A flood of sunlight bathed the hotel grounds late one afternoon. Joseph got his rifle from his room, then took a boat and rowed to an inlet out of the hotel's view. His eyes were keenly attuned to the sight of frogs, immediately seeing a half dozen among rocks and branches. He drew the oars into the boat and reached for the rifle, but instead of shouldering it, he placed it on his lap as he sat hunched on the middle seat. For weeks he had a feeling that his killing was senseless, that he was carrying out a promise simply because he had made it in a moment of high emotion. The forces that had inspired him at the beginning of the summer were gone. Prolonging the massacres, in the belief that he was somehow avenging the survivors at the hotel, was nonsense.

From the events he had witnessed between his father and Zushe, he had learned to accept adults with their flaws. He had learned the power of forgiveness and the futility of living in the past. The act of killing frogs meant he was living in the past, in a world that was not his, that was nobody's. Surely, he had to remember—never to forget what had been done to the Jews—but to kill in the name of that belief was not for him. He grasped the wooden rifle-butt with both hands, letting the barrel rest on the rim of the boat, angled down towards the water. He let the rifle dip lower and lower. The butt slipped slowly through his hands, then with a low, muffled sound, the rifle vanished into the lake. For a long time, Joseph sat contemplating his gift.

Beryl was feeling stronger by the day. One morning he called to Freda from the back lawn. The proprietress stepped out through the kitchen door, wiping her hands on her apron as she shuffled towards Beryl.

"Next year I'm going to plant a vegetable garden right here," he promised, staking out a plot with broad gestures of his arms. "Tomatoes, cabbage, green pepper, and maybe even cauliflower. No, not cauliflower—it makes gas."

"If the children don't trample it to pieces," she replied.

"We'll have to build a fence around it, of course," he stated, refusing to let his enthusiasm wane. "I'll come at the end of June—maybe even earlier."

"That's fine with me. Maybe at the same time you'll clean up the winter debris from the front lawn?"

"Why not, if I'm already here."

"Thank you, Beryl," she replied delightedly, as though the task had already been completed.

No one was surprised that Beryl was planning to leave the hotel on the Sabbath. In the morning he met Joseph on the patio. He feigned a smile to conceal his weariness.

"Have you been working on the Kaplansky book?" he asked.

"Not very much."

"There's still time—no rush," he said, concealing

his disappointment beneath a grin. A child's shoe lay on the sand below them. Beryl pointed it out to Joseph. "Shoes," he whispered sadly. "When Auschwitz was liberated, they found sixty thousand pairs of children's shoes, all neatly arranged by size. Nazi orderliness! The world complimented them for it!" He gazed into Joseph's eyes. "The world must be forced to remember this—and that's your job, because you're a writer."

There was a momentary silence in which Beryl met Joseph's eyes.

"There's something I wanted to tell you these last few weeks. You remember how Kaplansky died?" Joseph nodded. "He was shot in the back." Beryl paused, his eyes averted, as if reviewing that fateful scene in the forest. "It could have been me. No," he murmured. "It was me. I killed him. It was an accident, but it was I who killed him."

"It was an accident," Joseph said in a palliative tone.

"I killed him," came the slow knell-like sound of Beryl's confession.

Mid-afternoon, a taxi turned into the hotel driveway. Beryl's wife was waiting on the front lawn with their baggage. From the dock, Sollie saw Beryl carrying his valise down the patio steps. He shuffled hurriedly across the front lawn to bid Beryl farewell. Beryl could not restrain a smile on seeing Sollie waddle towards him. He took Sollie's bulbous hand and held it, smiling.

"Sollie, you have to promise to lose fifty pounds over the winter."

"I will, I promise."

"Sollie, you're a liar! You always were!"

They embraced loosely, Beryl's arms barely reaching beyond Sollie's hips.

"Be happy," Sollie said.

"I'm always happy."

Suddenly Zushe appeared. Although it grieved him that Beryl was about to desecrate the Sabbath by driving, he extended his hand to him. Beryl took it.

"Have a safe trip," Zushe said, "and may God bless you with good health and peace."

Beryl blinked his eyes to acknowledge the blessing, but remained silent, avoiding Zushe's eyes.

The hotel was almost deserted. Only one waiter remained to serve the meals. Zushe helped him. Mr. Dimant felt uncomfortable sitting at the table while Zushe served, so he stood up to take the plates from the rabbi's hands.

On the last day of the season, a group of guests met in the lobby for the morning prayers. When it was time to read from the Torah scroll, Zushe called Sollie, but he refused to accept the honour.

"I'm not a good Jew. I don't deserve to touch the Torah," he stammered, on the verge of tears.

Zushe was deeply moved by his words. He took Sollie by the arm and led him up to the makeshift dais in the corner of the lobby.

"Here, take my prayer shawl in your hands and touch the scroll with it," he instructed him.

Reluctantly, Sollie agreed to do it. With tears streaming down his cheeks, he recited the benediction he had not said since the summer of 1939.

The chessplayers were packed and waiting for a taxi. A wind from the lake played havoc with the professor's mane. It had never bothered him before, but today he had to keep his hair down.

"It's okay, it's okay," Mr. Dimant assured him as the professor kept both hands over his ears.

Zushe approached to wish them farewell.

"Will you be back next summer?" asked Mr. Dimant.

"Perhaps," he answered.

"Tell us something we can remember you by until we meet again," Mr. Dimant suggested. "Anything at all." Zushe smiled. "Come here, Shpitzer—stop worrying about your hair—it's not going to fly away."

After a moment of deliberation, Zushe pronounced slowly: "To be a realist, one must believe in miracles."

The aphorism impressed the two men. Professor Shpitzer grinned broadly while Mr. Dimant gave a grating little laugh.

"That's a good one! I'll remember that!" he cackled loudly.

At last the taxi arrived. He took Professor Shpitzer's hand and brought it to his lips. Zushe closed the door for them and bade them farewell.

A man and a boy stood on a hillock near the tracks overlooking the hotel. Fallen birch leaves lay in variegated heaps between the trees. In a few minutes Joseph would start on his return journey to Montreal. Zushe would stay on another day to help the kitchen staff close up for the winter.

"Two men may be close together physically, yet far apart," Zushe said in a voice that was solemn, but laden with emotion. "Men duelling stand back to back, touching each other, yet no two men can be farther apart. It can also happen that two men who are far apart physically are close to each other in spirit, so close that they can always feel each other's presence."

Joseph nodded, his long hair that had not been cut all summer waving across his brow and eyes.

"Where will you go from here?" Joseph asked.

"I'm not sure."

"Montreal?"

"Probably. With God's help."

"Will you visit me?"

"Of course."

"Joseph! Joseph!" Freda's voice was heard from the front lawn. "The taxi is here!"

"You better go," Zushe whispered, touching him on the arm.

Joseph felt a twinge of pain in his chest. He fought it off with a deep breath, holding himself stiffly against the wind. He extended his hand to Zushe, who took it with a smile. Gazing hopefully into the boy's eyes, Zushe asked, "Will you ever forgive me?"

The boy's moist, eager eyes answered: Yes, yes, of course.

Zushe opened his arms cautiously to the boy, and Joseph stepped into the embrace—but only for a moment—then he turned away abruptly and darted down the hill, bent forward, in full stride, his open jacket billowing high over his shoulders.

Abraham Boyarsky is a writer and a professor of mathematics at Concordia University in Montreal. His previous books, *A Pyramid of Time*, *Shreiber*, and *The Number Hall*, were great critical successes. Boyarsky has been honoured with the Writers Union of Canada's Gerald Lampert Award for a writer at the beginning of his career and the Jewish Book Committee's award for excellence in fiction.